Things had just gott dangerous.

Two shooting incidents, a wounded shoulder. She should get a customer loyalty card at the doc's.

She didn't know whether to laugh or cry. She did neither. She turned to Elijah. "If it'll make my aunt safer, I'll take your advice and go to your ranch."

"It'll make things safer for you, too."

"You don't know that. Nobody knows what's happening." She heard the shakiness in her voice.

How long was this going to go on? She was sick of being afraid. Tired of seeing other people get hurt. Angry enough to fight back. But she didn't know how. And she didn't know where to strike.

"It's going to be all right," he told her.

All right? The scrapes on her hand and face from getting thrown down on the asphalt stung. Her head pounded. She was so tired she could barely move. She couldn't stop trembling.

Fear and helplessness gnawed at her. This was never going to end. Not until the shooter got what he wanted.

Jenna Night comes from a family of Southern-born natural storytellers. Her parents were avid readers and the house was always filled with books. No wonder she grew up wanting to tell her own stories. She's lived on both coasts, but currently resides in the Inland Northwest where she's astonished by the occasional glimpse of a moose, a herd of elk or a soaring eagle.

Books by Jenna Night

Love Inspired Suspense

Last Stand Ranch

LAST STAND RANCH

JENNA NIGHT

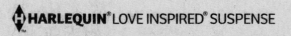

HARLEQUIN® LOVE INSPIRED® SUSPENSE

Recycling programs for this product may not exist in your area.

LOVE INSPIRED BOOKS

ISBN-13: 978-0-373-67742-9

Last Stand Ranch

This edition published by arrangement with Love Inspired Books.

www.Harlequin.com

Printed in U.S.A.

Peace I leave with you, my peace I give unto you:
not as the world giveth, give I unto you.
Let not your heart be troubled, neither let it be afraid.
–John 14:27

To my mom, Esther. Thanks for the faith!

Acknowledgments

Thank you editor Elizabeth Mazer for selecting me to be
on your team in the Love Inspired Suspense Killer Voices
contest. Your encouragement and stellar editing skills
are much appreciated. Yay, Team Elizabeth!

Thank you agent Sarah E. Younger
for your guidance and for making the pathway
to publication clearer. Yay, Team Sarah!

ONE

Olivia Dillon gripped the steering wheel of her sedan tighter and pressed the accelerator a little harder. She didn't want to drive recklessly, but Las Vegas, Nevada, and the threat to her life were only two hundred and fifty miles behind her.

She'd left the busy interstate twenty minutes ago, turning onto a quieter county highway that snaked gradually upward through scrubby Arizona high desert. To her right and left, shadowy rust-colored mesas towered like thunderheads in the distance. Straight ahead, the crumbly strip of asphalt angled sharply upward.

When summoning the courage to leave Vegas, she'd promised herself she would be at her great-aunt's ranch in Painted Rock, Arizona, before dark. That wasn't going to happen. Jamming the last few items from the apartment she'd just vacated into her rented storage space had taken longer than expected. Now the sun barely clung above the horizon to the west and she still had several more miles to go.

"It will be okay," she told herself for probably the hundredth time today. Not that she believed it.

She continued on, covering another twenty miles and gaining close to a thousand feet in elevation. The sun dropped off the edge of the world and the surrounding purple dusk took on a darker tinge.

She arrived at the edge of the tree line marking the start of rich northern Arizona forest, so she must be on the right track. A few more miles and the highway would intersect with the turnoff for Painted Rock, the only town for miles.

A flicker of light in the rearview mirror drew her attention to a set of car headlights in the gray distance behind her. It was the first car she'd seen since leaving the interstate.

She turned her gaze back to the road in front of her.

A few minutes later, a flicker of light in the mirror caught her eye again. She was startled to see the car had covered half the distance between them. That wasn't possible. Not unless the driver was going over a hundred miles an hour.

Well, she'd just get out of the way. The guy was probably drunk. She scanned the side of the road up ahead, looking for a place to pull over.

But she'd just entered the forest and there was nowhere she could go. No breakdown lane. No service roads.

Nervous, fluttery fear shifted anxiously in her chest. What if the driver didn't see her? What if he glanced at a text message just as he came upon her? Her life could be over in an instant. Here, in the middle of nowhere instead of in Las Vegas. How ironic that would be.

She glanced in the mirror to see how close the car was now.

Bright white high-beam headlights suddenly flashed on just inches behind her rear window. She jumped in surprise. The fluttery fear in her chest was now a frantic, clawing animal.

It had to be a truck or an SUV behind her. The headlights were high enough to bore through her back window and blind her to the road ahead. Terrified she'd career off the road, she tapped her brakes. The vehicle behind her smacked her bumper hard and her head snapped back against her headrest. Then the vehicle backed off.

Eerie, constantly shifting shadows danced through the inside of her sedan before her car interior suddenly lit up again. Another hard smack to her bumper jolted her. The light suddenly shifted to the side. Now what?

The tormenting vehicle passed her and shot off toward the darkness ahead only to stop suddenly, the taillights glaring at her like a pair of angry red eyes. The truck made a quick U-turn and headed back toward her.

This wasn't some random jerk who was drunk or high. This was someone deliberately out to hurt her. It had to be Ted Kurtz. The man who had promised to kill her. She let go a sound that was halfway between hysterical laughter and a terrified sob.

Just three weeks ago he'd warned her that her life wasn't worth much.

"It will be okay," she whispered, tired of the whole thing, drained by weeks of fear and exhausted by the sheer will it had taken to leave the safety of her apartment and take this trip.

The headlights grew nearer, and then suddenly they were right in front of her, in her lane and bearing down fast. Blinded again by the bright light, she didn't know what to do.

At the last second before impact, Olivia wrenched her steering wheel hard to the right. For the span of a couple of heartbeats she felt an odd, peaceful silence. Then her car was spinning sideways, careening over thick grass, scraping its undercarriage over chunks of rock, snapping the branches off pine trees and tossing up dirt in an arc all around her.

When she finally came to a stop, she continued to clutch the steering wheel for a long time.

She was still alive. *Thank You, Lord. Thank You. Thank You.* The words tumbled over and over in her mind. Not a prayer, exactly, but the closest she'd come to one in a while.

The dirt she'd stirred up slowly settled. She was facing the direction she'd just come from. Her engine had cut off, but both her headlights were still working.

She sat for a moment in the stillness, frozen in place. Images of what could have happened, what might still happen, flashed through her mind. Jagged, twisted metal. An explosion flaring into a fireball in the night sky. Herself just, well, gone.

The sound of her own shallow, uneven breaths brought her back to the moment. All too familiar with how controlling fear could be, she forced herself to move her arms a little and turn her head. Her muscles felt watery. The heavy, thudding pulse in the pit of her stomach made it hard to take a deep breath. But she forced herself to do it.

Her foot was jammed against the brake pedal. She lifted it and flexed it. Sore, but not sprained.

She looked around, able to see for a few car lengths directly in front of her but for only a foot or two to each side and behind.

Her attacker could still be out there. Ted Kurtz or maybe some crackhead thug he'd hired to kill her. She needed to get out of here before he came back.

With shaking hands she turned the key. The engine groaned but wouldn't restart.

She checked her phone. No service.

The heavy pulse in the center of her gut thumped harder. And faster.

What options did she have? Get out of her car and hike down the road until she picked up a phone signal? That didn't sound very appealing.

Or she could stay in her car and wait for help. A sitting duck. An easy target for someone wanting to come back and finish the job.

Hiking down the road was starting to sound like the better option. She could run if she saw someone coming or hide in the woods. Not an ideal situation, but it beat cowering in her car.

She'd been so shocked and terrified on that sidewalk back in Las Vegas, when Kurtz suddenly appeared at her side, smiling snidely while promising to catch her alone and kill her someday. Too stunned to collect herself in time to call out for help from the people passing by. After he walked away she could only take a few fumbling steps around the corner before her knees buckled and she'd slid to the concrete. Helpless. All she'd done was whimper.

Afterward, she'd promised herself she would never let fear do that to her again.

Now she summoned up what little bit of stubborn courage she had left and tucked her phone into her front pocket. She grabbed her wallet from her purse and shoved it in her back pocket. Then she set a couple unopened cans of soda in the center of her jacket and twisted it. Not the best weapon in the world, but better than nothing.

She shoved hard against the dented, protesting door, climbed out and crouched down low, pressing against the side of the car and balancing on the balls of her feet. Just in case. If that had been Kurtz driving, he could be watching her every movement right now. He was a crack shot. He'd mentioned that in his testimony in court.

Stop stalling.

A deep breath, and then… She heard something. The sound of an engine. In the distance, lights flickered between the trees. But something didn't look right. They weren't car headlights.

A motorcycle appeared at the turn in the highway. Then another, and another. In the illumination spilling from their headlights she could see the riders wore leather vests with some sort of patches. Colors, she'd heard them called. Gangs wore them.

A biker gang? Seriously? Someone drove by when she desperately needed help and it was *these* guys? She stayed crouched down low.

The first rider roared past her. A dozen more filed by after him. Should she ask them for help?

The decision was made for her. The rider in the front slowed, made a U-turn across the highway, and then headed back. He rode up closer to her and stopped. Then he put his hand down to the side and made a backing motion. The other riders came to a stop a few yards away. He killed his engine.

Now what? There was no point in hiding, so she stood. Her calf muscles registered a cramped, painful protest.

He pulled off his helmet and rested it on his thigh. "Need some help?" He stayed seated on his chopper. His hair was dark and short, almost a military cut. His eyes were hidden in the shadows cast by the other riders' headlights.

He didn't smile, but his tone was friendly enough. The fact that he wasn't trying to charm her made him seem somewhat more trustworthy.

At this point, what did she have to lose? "I had a little trouble," she said.

He nodded. "I can see that."

"And I can't get reception on my phone."

He kicked out the kickstand on his motorcycle and stood up. Medium height. Medium build. Not a huge guy, but there was something imposing about the way he moved, nevertheless. He swung a leg over his bike and started toward her, his heavy boots crunching atop the loose gravel on the road. She was already pressed up against her car or she would have backed up. He finally stopped a couple of paces away from her, reached a leather-gloved hand into his pocket and pulled out a small satellite phone. He glanced at the screen. "Here, my phone's working."

She hesitated to close the gap between them. But if he meant her harm, why would he go through such an elaborate act? She reached for the phone, her trembling hand betraying her fear. "Thanks." The wallpaper on the screen was a black oval with a silver sword in the middle. Beneath it were the words *Vanquish the Darkness*. Olivia had no idea what that meant. She wasn't about to ask.

The woman was in trouble and Elijah could tell it went well beyond her battered car. He'd spotted her crouched by the car, eyes wide with fear, looking like a cornered coyote ready to bolt.

Elijah continually scanned his surroundings, paid attention to small details and saw a lot of things other people never noticed. "Head on a swivel" was the term they'd used over in the sandbox. The practice of looking everywhere, all the time, was a skill he'd first learned in Iraq and later used in Afghanistan. A habit that had kept him alive, and one he didn't plan to ever lose.

The woman watched him warily while she looked up a contact on her own phone and then punched the numbers into his. He didn't mean her harm, but she didn't know that. He'd left his phone on speaker and she didn't change the setting, so a few seconds later he was surprised to hear a familiar voice say, "Elijah, honey, is that you?"

The woman stared at him, eyes widened. Her jaw dropped slightly. "Aunt Claudia?" she finally said into the phone. "Is that *you*?"

There was a pause, and then, "Olivia?"

"Yes!"

Elijah could practically see relief cascading over Olivia as her shoulders relaxed.

Olivia. So this was the grandniece Claudia Sweeney had been telling everyone in town about for the past two weeks. The first blood relative to come visit the eighty-year-old woman in as long as Elijah could remember. Of course she was bringing trouble with her. She hadn't seen fit to visit her great-aunt in the past, which meant she was probably here now because she wanted something.

He watched her shift her weight back and forth, nervously glancing up and down the highway. She was trying to outrun some kind of trouble, which meant she was bringing it to the doorstep of a woman who'd always treated

Elijah like family. If her problems caused harm to Claudia, she was going to find herself moving on a lot sooner than she thought.

"Are you already here in town?" Claudia asked.

"Not yet," Olivia answered. "I'm still on the highway." She glanced back toward her car. "I've had some trouble."

"What kind of trouble?" Concern was evident in the way Claudia carefully spoke each word. "And why are you calling on Elijah Morales's phone?"

Olivia turned back to face Elijah and moved the phone slightly away from her face. "Is your name Elijah Morales?"

He nodded once.

"Do you know my great-aunt Claudia?"

"Claudia Sweeney? Yes."

She knit her brows together. "*How* do you know her?"

"We're neighbors. And we go to church together."

She stared at him, and then turned her gaze to his buddies before finally turning back to him.

"Do *all* of you guys go to church with my aunt?" She strung out the words, hesitating between each one, as if they didn't quite make sense when she put them together.

Elijah felt one corner of his mouth twitch

slightly upward with the hint of a half smile.
Yes, he was well aware that they didn't look like
your typical church group. For himself, he certainly wasn't pretty as a picture. The scars on
his face were small, but people noticed them.
Some of his fellow riders looked a little rough,
too. He chose his friends based on their charac-
ter and gave no thought to how they looked to
anyone else. But how do you explain that in a
few quick seconds to a woman who looks as if
she's on the verge of panic?

You don't.

He glanced at her car jammed up against a
sapling that had nearly snapped in half, and then
he looked back at her. "It's a crazy world."

She actually laughed. Only once, but it seemed
to help calm her. Eventually he would press her
a little harder for details on what had happened.
Right now he just wanted to help her hold it together, assist her with her car and get her someplace safe.

"Olivia!" Through the phone, Claudia was
trying to get her attention.

"I'm here," Olivia mumbled, sounding dazed.

"Why don't you hand the phone back to Elijah? Let me talk to him and find out where you
are so I can figure out what we need to do."

"Okay." Olivia held out the phone to Elijah.
"She wants to talk to you."

"I'll have your niece on her way as soon as I can," Elijah said into the phone.

"Would you take me off speaker?"

"Sure." He hit the button. "You're off speaker."

"Is she really all right?" Claudia asked.

Elijah wondered that himself as he started walking around her car to take a closer look. The glow from a dozen motorcycle headlights gave him a pretty decent view. There were the expected scrapes and scratches along the sides of the car that probably came from the rocks and trees once she'd gone off road. But there were dents on the back bumper, too.

"She seems all right," he said into the phone. "Her car's wrecked, though. One of us needs to hang up and call Ricky so he can fire up his tow truck and get her car."

"I'll do that right now," Claudia said.

After they disconnected, he walked down the highway looking for the spot where Olivia's car had left the road.

He found it. It looked as if Olivia had turned off the road deliberately. If there were skid marks showing she'd tried to brake, it was too dark to see them.

"A tow truck will be here soon," he said when he got back to her. "Want to tell me what happened?"

"I ran off the road." She turned away, suddenly very interested in looking everywhere but at him.

She was hiding something.

Elijah would have to find out what that was. Claudia Sweeney might be Olivia's blood relative, but she'd been Elijah's neighbor for his entire life. He was not about to let anything happen to her. Painted Rock was full of people he cared about. If trouble was coming to his town, he wanted to know about it.

TWO

As soon as Olivia's car was loaded onto the flatbed of the tow truck and Olivia was safely stowed in the cab with Ricky, Elijah's fellow riders headed for their homes while Elijah rode ahead to Claudia's house to wait for Olivia's arrival. He wasn't leaving until he knew exactly what was going on.

"It's a shame Olivia had car trouble on top of everything else," Claudia said quietly.

"Yes, ma'am," Elijah agreed. He didn't know what "everything else" was, but he would find out.

He was sitting on his motorcycle in front of Claudia's house, a frontier Victorian with pink, yellow and lavender gingerbread. Claudia stood near the bottom of the wooden steps leading to the wraparound porch. At just over six feet tall, Claudia's regal bearing hadn't been stooped by the advancing years. But it had turned her formerly auburn hair to silver. She wore it tied in a loose bun, like usual, but in honor of her niece's visit, she'd dressed up in a long denim skirt and a red flowery blouse. Two of her dogs, Jasper and Feldspar, sat by her feet while the third, Opal, nosed around a flower bed.

"So you and the guys were just out riding and happened to come across Olivia?" Claudia asked.

"We were coming back from a home visit. We dropped off a gift card to the grocery store, then rode around and gunned the engines a few times for the kids. I took the oldest kid for a short ride, we handed out a few toys and then we left. We were on our way back when I saw her."

The tow truck with Olivia's car finally turned into the circular drive. Elijah got off his bike and walked over to stand beside his adopted "aunt." She clenched her blue-veined hands with impatient excitement while waiting for Olivia to climb out of Ricky's tow truck. Elijah hadn't breathed a word of his wariness about her grandniece to her. She'd been so anxious for this moment, he didn't want to spoil it. Not unless he had to.

The tow truck squeaked to a stop and Olivia opened her cab door. Elijah strode over and offered up a hand to help her out.

"I can manage," she said tightly, so he stepped back.

Ricky hopped out of the driver's side of the

truck and started to pull Olivia's luggage from the compartment behind the cab.

Elijah grabbed a couple of bags. If that annoyed Olivia, too bad.

Olivia grabbed a duffel bag and frowned at him. "Thanks for your help, but I can take care of things from here."

She thought she could dismiss him? That was cute.

He walked beside her across the drive and caught her biting her bottom lip when she saw an Oso County Sheriff's Department patrol car pull in.

Ricky had called for a deputy while they were still out on the highway. Olivia had stepped away to talk to the lawman when he arrived, so Elijah hadn't been able to hear their conversation. Deputy Bedford was newly assigned to Painted Rock. He'd been pretty closemouthed after talking to Olivia, walking around with a flashlight and looking at her car and at the surface of the road.

Since it was impossible to see very far down the winding road in the darkness, even using the spotlight on his patrol car, Bedford had wanted to drive down the highway and look for skid marks or debris. He'd told them he'd meet them at Claudia's house to wrap up the incident.

Elijah and Olivia reached the bottom of the porch steps and set down their bags.

"You made it!" Claudia cried out in delight, wrapping her arms around her niece and rocking her slightly from side to side.

"Finally." Olivia's voice was muffled as she obediently stayed wrapped in her great-aunt's enthusiastic embrace.

Elijah couldn't see any resemblance between them. Claudia, with her big bones and impressive height, towered over Olivia, who was average height, but scrawny looking.

Ricky yelled out "good-bye" as he jumped back in his truck and headed for his garage with Olivia's car.

Deputy Bedford got out of his patrol car carrying a clipboard.

"Good evening, Mrs. Sweeney." He nodded at Claudia as he walked up. Claudia and Olivia were still at the bottom of the porch steps, each with an arm wrapped around the other. Elijah noticed Claudia tightening her hold on her niece as the deputy came closer.

"I saw some fresh skid marks on the road that came from wider tires than yours, just as you described," Bedford said. Olivia nodded.

"Any chance there's a bigger story you want to tell me?" Bedford added.

"What do you mean?"

Bedford looked at her for a moment. "Someone taps your bumper twice, passes you, then comes back and forces you off the highway. That doesn't sound like an accident. That sounds personal. Who would do that? And why?"

Those were the questions Elijah wanted to ask.

"Someone threatened to kill me back in Las Vegas," Olivia said. "Maybe the guy who drove me off the road tonight was him. Maybe not." She glanced at Claudia, her eyebrows raised in an unspoken plea for understanding. "I'd hoped I'd get away from him here, but now it looks like I'll have to move on."

So that was why Olivia had come to Painted Rock. She was running for her life. And potentially putting Claudia in harm's way.

Deputy Bedford cocked his head slightly to one side. "Who was the man who threatened your life?"

"His name is Ted Kurtz. He's an attorney in Las Vegas."

"The man you testified against? I ran your name through the computer. As soon as I saw the pictures, I recognized you from the news stories on TV."

Olivia had been on TV? Las Vegas was less than three hundred miles away. If anything made the news there, it usually made the news in Painted Rock. But Elijah didn't have much time for TV. "What happened?" he asked.

Olivia glared at him. Then she turned back to the deputy and lifted her chin, as if daring him to take his best shot. She was tough. Elijah had to give her that. She might have looked terrified crouching by her car out on the highway, but she'd looked determined then, too.

"I worked at a safe house for battered women in Las Vegas," Olivia said, her voice flat and emotionless. "We had a woman stay with us on three different occasions over the course of about six months. Eventually she told us her name, Marion Kurtz, and that her husband was Ted Kurtz. He's a big-shot defense attorney with links to organized crime."

Her gaze shifted to something just beyond Elijah's shoulder. Sorrow filled her eyes and the defiant line of her lips slackened. Elijah knew from experience what was happening. She was looking into the past.

"We tried to get Marion into counseling, get her out of danger, get her to file a police report and press charges. She'd show some interest, but then she wouldn't follow through." Olivia's voice began to waver a little. "Finally, Marion came in with a black eye, a broken nose and a split lip. She said she was ready to press charges and leave her husband."

Elijah dreaded hearing where her story might go.

"But she didn't leave him and she never filed a police report. She decided to give him one more chance after he promised he would change. A week later Marion ended up in the hospital ICU, unconscious for two days." Olivia's voice caught, and she stopped talking for a few seconds to clear her throat. "When she regained consciousness, she claimed it had been a random attack. But later, she told me her husband had done it. She wouldn't repeat that to the police, though, because Ted told her she wouldn't survive if she did. He'd defended people in court who owed him favors. People who could make her disappear."

Claudia reached over to brush the hair from Olivia's face. "Honey, given the situation, no one can blame you for what you did."

Olivia looked up at her. "If it hadn't been for you..." Her voice trailed off and she shook her head. "I knew his alibi was a complete lie," she continued. "I wanted to make any potential jurors question it, so when I testified before the grand jury, so they could determine whether the case would go to trial, I claimed I saw him at a time and place when I actually didn't."

"Oh, honey." Claudia shook her head.

"I *saw* Marion in the hospital. I saw what he did to her. I was angry and I wanted to do something to make sure he wouldn't be able to hurt her again." Olivia shoved her hands in her pockets. "I regretted the lie almost as soon as I told it. A few days later I retracted my statement."

She turned to Elijah. "Without enough evidence to move forward with the trial, the charges against Kurtz were dropped. Charges were filed against me, but they were eventually dropped, too. Marion had permanent hearing loss and some other physical issues, but she did file for divorce. Things looked like they were blowing over.

"Then three weeks ago Kurtz came up to me while I was walking down a sidewalk. I didn't see him coming—he was just suddenly there beside me. He told me he was going to kill me. Things hadn't blown over for him. Old rumors about him had taken on a new life. Stories that he was violent, that his hair-trigger temper made him unhinged. That he'd hurt people before.

"The law firm where he works has to maintain a thin veneer of respectability and they were angry with him for marring that. His future there is in question, even now. He told me that getting rid of me would send a message to the women he's hurt in the past about the consequences of standing up to him." Her voice was hard with bitterness now, and shimmering tears were forming in the corners of her eyes.

"That's why you're here?" Elijah asked. "To get away from him?"

Olivia nodded. "Aunt Claudia saw me on TV during the worst of it and called me. She invited me to come for a visit, but I could barely bring myself to leave my apartment." She impatiently rubbed her eyes, smearing away the tears that lingered there. "I lost my job after I told the truth. I was hoping to start a new life here."

Silence followed. Finally, Bedford spoke. "Are you sure you've told me the truth about what happened on the road?"

"I'm not making it up."

"You do realize Ted Kurtz probably bills his clients in the neighborhood of a thousand bucks an hour? Can you really imagine him taking the time to personally trail you all the way from Las Vegas to Painted Rock just to bump your car a few times and drive you off the road?"

"I never said I was sure it was him. Maybe he hired someone."

"What's *your* theory?" Elijah asked Bedford.

He wasn't thrilled that Olivia had brought trouble to Claudia's house, but it sounded as if she did have a good reason to fear for her life. Now Bedford wanted to dismiss everything she'd said, leaving her alone and vulnerable, just because she'd made a bad decision in the past?

Bedford held up a hand. "I don't have a theory. I want to help." He glanced at Claudia. "Right now I'm just collecting the facts. Trying to figure out what to believe. And Miss Dillon has a track record of not telling the truth."

He was interrupted by a radio transmission and stepped away to respond through his collar mic. "Dispatch says a couple of calls have come in about someone driving erratically on the highway," he said when he came back. "But given your history, I can't ask Las Vegas PD to go to Ted Kurtz's home to see if he's there based solely on your word. Are you sure you can't tell me anything about the driver or the vehicle?"

"It was a dark-colored truck. His lights were even with my back window. I don't have any more details. I couldn't see very well."

"There's not much I can do with that." Bedford took a business card from his clipboard and jotted a number on the back. "Here's your incident report number. You'll be able to access the report by eight o'clock tomorrow morning."

Olivia took the card.

"Good night," Bedford said, and he left.

"I can stay here tonight if you'd like," Elijah said to Claudia.

After Deputy Bedford drove off, they'd walked into the house. Olivia watched Elijah wrap an arm around Claudia's shoulder as they stood in her kitchen. It was an easy gesture that made Olivia give herself a swift mental kick. She was the one who should have that relaxed, familiar relationship with her great-aunt. She should have visited Claudia years ago. She shouldn't have waited until she had no other options.

"That's okay, honey." Claudia patted Elijah on the arm. "We've got the dogs, and they're the best alarm I could have. Plus, Denise and Raymond are in the cottage out back." She turned to Olivia. "They're the couple I hired to help me run the place. Here, let me text them and tell them you're here so you can meet them." She picked up a phone and started tapping the screen. "Don't worry," she said, glancing up at Elijah. "We'll be fine."

"It wouldn't be any trouble to stay," Elijah said. "You know I'd like nothing more than to hang around here and take care of my favorite aunt."

"Laying it on a little thick, aren't you?" Olivia

groused. She hadn't meant to say that out loud, but where did he get off calling Claudia "aunt"?

Elijah grinned at Olivia and hugged Claudia tighter.

Seriously? That's how it was going to be? After everything she'd been through tonight, he was going to needle her? He still looked tough, but now that they were inside and in better light, she could see a hint of mischief in his dark eyes. It was already getting on her nerves.

"I think we'll be okay." Olivia glanced at the windows she would lock and the shades she would pull before going to bed. She would go through the whole house, checking and double-checking that everything was secure. It was part of the ritual that helped her sleep at night.

"I don't mind staying." Elijah's bantering tone was gone in an instant. The mischievous glint in his eyes was replaced with a look like cold black ice. "I'd love to be here if he decides to stop by."

Olivia's attention was drawn to the sound of a woman's voice just before she heard a door open. It was followed by the sound of footsteps.

"That'll be Denise and Raymond," Claudia said, leading the way into the kitchen.

"I hope I didn't interrupt your dinner," Claudia called out to a woman with glossy, chocolate-colored hair, who stood holding a small basket heaped with corn-bread muffins. A man with shoulder-length, sun-streaked brown hair stood beside her.

"Oh, no." The woman, who looked as if she might be a decade older than Olivia, smiled broadly. "Raymond and I finished eating a while ago. I baked a full dozen muffins when I made our supper and thought you and your guest might like a few of them."

"Thank you." Claudia took the basket and set it on the counter. "I'd like you to meet my great-niece, Olivia."

"I'm glad to finally meet you," Denise said. "It's so nice of you to come for a visit."

Olivia exchanged glances with Claudia. Apparently her aunt hadn't felt the need to explain the real motivation for her trip to Painted Rock. "Nice to be here," Olivia mumbled.

"Heard you had some trouble on the road," the man standing beside Denise commented.

Olivia wasn't sure what to say in response. It wasn't a conversation she wanted to have with another stranger.

"Raymond keeps things up and running around here," Claudia interjected.

"I'm looking forward to seeing the ranch in the morning," Olivia said.

Claudia wrapped an arm around her shoulder. "I'll bet right now you just want to take a nice hot bath, crawl into bed and get some rest."

It was exactly what she wanted.

"Time for us to go," Denise said to Raymond. She glanced at Olivia. "We just wanted to pop in and welcome you. We'll see you in the morning."

"You hungry?" Claudia asked after they left.

"Starved."

"Denise made fried chicken for supper, but we put it in the fridge after you called from the side of the highway to tell me you'd run into trouble. Shall we have a cold supper and turn in?"

Olivia nodded.

"You go on home," Claudia said to Elijah. "I'll keep my phone turned on and by my side all night."

Olivia frowned at Elijah, hoping he would leave. She wouldn't be able to relax with him around. Not with those muscular arms under that black T-shirt distracting her. Plus the fact that just about every time she looked at him, he was already looking at her. The dream of finally being able to let down her guard, even if just for a short while, was what fueled her determination to leave Las Vegas and make the drive here.

"I live close by," Elijah said to her after a long pause. "My family's ranch borders Aunt Claudia's property. I can get here fast if I need to."

Olivia nodded. Good to know.

"All right, I'll head on home." He turned to

Claudia. "Call me if you hear anything. And make sure you lock your doors."

"Of course."

Elijah headed out of the kitchen, across the dining area and toward the front door. The women walked with him.

He paused as he passed through the front room and glanced toward something on a bookshelf. Olivia followed his glaze and saw a framed photograph of an older gentleman with a long rectangular face, thick white hair and gigantic sideburns. He looked familiar. Olivia walked toward the picture.

"My Hugh," Claudia said quietly, stepping up behind Olivia.

"Of course." Aunt Claudia and Uncle Hugh had made a trip to Phoenix for a visit when Olivia was fourteen. She remembered now that Hugh was about a foot shorter than Claudia. She'd said hello to them and then scampered off to the mall with her friends. Hugh had died a few years later of a sudden massive heart attack.

"What's this?" Olivia asked, pointing to something brittle and crumbling in the lower right corner of the frame, underneath the glass.

Claudia laughed softly. "Hugh picked that daisy and gave it to me the morning he passed away. Of course it came from a flower bed that

I tended." Claudia touched the glass. "He was something, all right."

Elijah hesitated instead of continuing out the door. Olivia was afraid he'd change his mind and stay. "It was good to meet you," he finally said to Olivia. "Sorry about the circumstances."

She nodded, willing him to go. He might be Claudia's protector, but he wasn't hers.

The second he was out the door she snapped the dead bolt into place. The porch light was already on. In the gap between the curtains and the window frame she could see light reflecting off his motorcycle as he climbed on and cranked up the engine.

Let the knight in chrome armor go rescue somebody else. Olivia Dillon was on her own. Especially now that she knew leaving Las Vegas hadn't made her any safer. She'd thought she could restart her life with a clean slate in Painted Rock, but that obviously wasn't going to happen. And there was no way she would put her great-aunt in danger.

She needed a new plan. Maybe Ricky the mechanic would give her a few bucks for her car. She could buy a bus ticket to a bigger city. Get lost in the crowd and stay in a shelter until she could find a job. She needed to run farther. And the sooner she left, the better.

THREE

Elijah's mom taught him to be respectful of the wishes of a woman, so when a woman asked him to do something, he always listened. But that didn't mean he always did what she asked.

The morning after finding Olivia by the side of the highway, he steered his dirt bike toward the back of Claudia's house. Just after sunrise most mornings, he could find Claudia there feeding her chickens, looking over her property and greeting the morning sun. He found her right where he expected, dressed in jeans and an orange-checked shirt and wearing an old pair of Hugh's battered blue suede house slippers.

Olivia stood next to her, slump-shouldered, looking like a withered blade of golden grass. When he drove up she glared at him through bloodshot eyes. Probably the result of a sleepless night. And yeah, he'd gotten the message—she wished he would stay away. Too bad. Sorry, Mom.

"Morning, honey," Claudia called out as he killed the engine. At least somebody was glad to see him.

"Good morning." He got off the bike.

Claudia walked over to him, one of her chubby little beagles by her feet. "Have you eaten breakfast? Denise made a pineapple bread pudding."

"Yes, ma'am, I already ate."

He turned to Olivia, who'd sullenly followed her aunt. "How are you this morning?" He reached down to scratch Jasper behind his ears. "Did you get any sleep?"

"A little."

A brittle spirit showed through in the pinched, angry expression on her face. Elijah knew that feeling well. He'd come home from Iraq and later Afghanistan fighting his own version of it.

It was likely she wanted to shove everyone away. It was a good thing she had Claudia, who was good at soothing hurts. Elijah's talent lay more in the realm of poking at whatever hurt until the person realized they wanted to lay down the hurt more than they wanted to coddle it. They appreciated his help in the long run. In the short run, not so much.

"Ricky told me it would take him at least a couple weeks to fix your car. I thought you might have gotten a ride to the bus station and moved on by now."

"It would probably be safer for *your* aunt if I did."

Boy, that "aunt" thing really bothered her. Too bad. Half the town referred to Claudia as "Aunt Claudia."

Claudia waved her hands. "That's enough of that talk about moving on." She turned to Olivia. "You're staying."

Elijah watched Olivia look down, then look off into the distance. She took a deep breath and her eyes filled with worry. Afraid to stay and afraid to go, most likely.

He turned his attention to Claudia. "I just stopped by to let you know I'll be working on that section of fence damaged in that last storm." He glanced at Olivia. "It's right at the boundary between Claudia's property and ours, not too far away."

She shrugged as if it meant nothing to her.

Then he made a point of pulling the pistol out of the waistband at the small of his back, and replacing it, as if he'd just wanted to make the fit more comfortable. Olivia kept her gaze on the gun the whole time. When she looked at him, it was with just a little bit less hostility.

Good. He wanted her to know at least one person took her fears of being stalked by Ted Kurtz seriously. Even if that person happened to be a guy she didn't much like.

"Before you got here, I was asking Olivia where she'd go if she didn't stay here with us," Claudia said.

"Good question." Elijah nodded. "Where *would* you go and how would you know when you were safe?"

"Wow." Olivia looked him up and down. "You really know how to make a girl feel better."

"Running off in a blind panic could make things a whole lot worse for you."

She hugged her arms over her chest. Elijah could see goose bumps on the surface of her skin even though she was standing in the sun.

"I'm so glad to have you here," Claudia said, reaching out to squeeze her niece's hand.

Oh, yeah, that. Sometimes Elijah forgot to say the warm fuzzy words. A fair amount of the time he couldn't say them because he didn't really believe them. But in this case he knew they were true. Claudia had been very excited about the visit.

"I'm glad to be here."

In the bright sunlight, Elijah could see the purple half circles under her eyes. Probably been missing out on sleep for a while. She was pale for a woman who lived in Vegas. And her clothes hung loosely on her. Whether she wanted to admit it or not, she needed all the help she could get.

"Your house is beautiful," Olivia said to Claudia, scanning the yard. Elijah watched her gaze settle on the junipers planted at the corners of the small guest cottage fifty feet away, current home of Raymond and Denise Bauer. Then she looked toward the numerous wooden sheds on the property, their interiors darkened and impossible to see into.

"You looking for Kurtz?" Elijah asked.

She snapped her attention back to Claudia, ignoring his question. "Painted Rock is such a pretty, peaceful town. It's everything I'd hoped for. I don't want to stay and ruin it for you."

"If you leave, you'll break an old lady's heart."

Olivia let go a laugh. "Please don't try to guilt me into staying."

"I will if it works. And don't forget about the job interview I lined up for you at the senior center. Are you going to throw away that opportunity after all the effort I put into getting it for you?"

"You're merciless." Olivia had already returned to scanning her surroundings. She looked toward Claudia's corrals and stables, worrying her bottom lip between her teeth.

"There's nobody out here," Claudia said, following her gaze.

For a moment, there was only the peaceful sound of the breeze rustling through the trees and chickens clucking as they moseyed around the yard.

"I've got too many dogs for anybody to sneak up on us," Claudia added.

"I don't know how much help Jasper, Feldspar and Opal would be as watchdogs," Elijah said.

Claudia shot him a quelling look. Unfortunately, it looked as if today was his day to annoy Claudia as well as Olivia. Claudia obviously wanted to wrap her niece in comfort and reassurance. Elijah didn't think that was a good idea. Not now. Not if it made her ignore the fact that she was still in danger.

Now that he knew more about the danger she was facing, he wasn't so anxious for her to leave town. He still didn't want Claudia at risk—but Olivia didn't deserve to be constantly on the run, either. Not when her only crime was crossing the line to try to help someone who'd been hurt.

"If you stay here," he added, "you'll have quite a few people looking out for you. If you take off running, you'll be alone. And it could be a very short run."

Olivia's eyes glistened. Claudia sniffed loudly and brought her hand to her mouth.

Oh, yeah, Elijah had quite the way with the ladies.

"I don't want to go," Olivia blurted out. "But I don't want to stay, either. Not if Ted Kurtz has tracked me here. And yet I'm so tired of hiding. It feels like I've been hiding forever."

"Right here, right this minute, we're fine." Claudia frowned at Elijah while she pulled a tissue out of her pocket and handed it to Olivia. "Sometimes we just have to focus on that."

Olivia drew in a deep breath and wiped her eyes and nose with the tissue.

Both women were upset and on edge. Elijah's work here was done. It was a shame doing the right thing didn't always make people feel good. But it might keep them alive.

"I've got to get to work on that fence," Elijah said to Claudia. "Call me if you have any trouble. Call 911, but have someone call me, too. I'll be closer. I'll get here faster."

"Okay." Claudia nodded.

Elijah climbed on his bike, cranked up the engine and headed back toward the Morales ranch. Mission accomplished. He'd found out what he'd wanted to know, he'd told the ladies what he'd wanted them to know and Olivia hadn't killed him with a look.

"I've got eleven hundred acres, most of it heading due east from here." Claudia pointed toward the far reaches of her ranch. "It joins up with federal parkland so there aren't any public roads for a long ways. Ted Kurtz couldn't sneak up on us from back here even if he was in the neighborhood."

Olivia gazed at the grassy land closest to the house, with stables, corrals and fenced pasture fanning out in every direction. The land to the north was rocky, forested foothills heading up into the mountains.

"Raymond will be out here doing his maintenance work and looking after what few animals I've got left." Claudia sighed softly. "This place used to be a lot busier, but after Hugh passed away I sold off most of the herd and started leasing out my grazing land."

"It's gorgeous." Olivia wondered why her parents never came to visit. How come her dad, Claudia's nephew, never brought her out here?

"Getting outside always raises my spirits." Claudia lifted her chin. "I've kept a few horses. Do you ride? I could saddle one up for you."

"I never learned how to ride." Until recently, Olivia didn't even realize she had a relative who owned horses.

"Well, now you'll have to stay around so you can learn."

In the quiet, they heard the rumble of Elijah's motorcycle growing fainter. "So, Elijah likes to get into other people's business?"

Claudia laughed. "He's been that way since he was a kid. He's always on the lookout for trouble, always wanting to take care of things. He was an army ranger. I think he must have been pretty good at it, too. But he said he missed his family's ranch after a few years and he came back home."

"I can see why he'd miss it. I wouldn't mind living in a place like this." Even though she couldn't help picking out potential spots where Ted Kurtz or some thug he'd hired might be hiding. She was being irrational; she knew it. Jumping at shadows wouldn't do her any good. Elijah was right, much as she hated to admit it. She had to make smart choices, be logical. But she also had to stop letting fear control her life. She had to stop letting *Ted Kurtz* control her life.

"Fresh air and sunshine will do you a world of good." Claudia leaned over to pull a weed from the flower bed. "I'm expecting a call—I've got to get back inside." She tossed the weed aside and wiped her hands on her jeans. "You're welcome to come back in the house with me or stay out here. Your choice."

Claudia was right. It really was her choice.

"You know what? I'm tired of being afraid." What kind of life did you have if you were afraid to go for a walk in the sun? "I think I will stay out here and meander around a little bit. Maybe I'll find Raymond and see if he can use some help."

"He's working in the stable this morning. He can always use a hand."

Claudia went back into the house and Olivia headed across the yard toward the stable, where she could hear Raymond working as she drew closer. On the way, she passed a large shed with the door propped open. She slowed down, hesitated to pass, but saw only some trucks and farm equipment inside. No Ted Kurtz waiting to jump out and get her.

What a drama queen she'd become.

Raymond had turned a couple of horses out in a corral while he lugged feed from the back of a truck into a storage building.

"Hello," Olivia called out.

Raymond started and spun toward her, a scowl slashed across his face. Then he stood and replaced the scowl with a thin smile. "Hello."

"Sorry, I didn't mean to startle you."

"Oh, it's my own fault." His smile strengthened as he wiped the sweat off his brow with his lower arm. "I heard about what happened to you on the highway last night. I guess it's made me a little jumpy."

"I feel like I've been jumpy forever." She scratched her thumbnail against a loose fleck of paint on the stable wall. "Could you use some help?"

"Sure. There are always things to do. But

don't you want to spend your time visiting with your aunt? Your vacation here will fly by before you know it."

"Actually, I'm thinking about staying in Painted Rock." Maybe her plan to get a new start here was back on again. There was no harm in mentioning it out loud and seeing how it felt. It felt pretty good.

"You think you might settle in here? Claudia must be thrilled. I wasn't sure she even had any living relatives until we found out you were coming for a visit."

Olivia felt a twinge of guilt. She scratched at the peeling paint a little harder. "Just something I'm thinking about."

"And you want me to put you to work?" He grinned. "You want me to help you figure out if you're cut out for ranch life?"

"Physical work might make me a little less jumpy."

"It probably will." He rubbed his hand across his chin while he looked around at the various sheds, stalls and other buildings on the property. "If you don't mind getting your hands dirty, I might have something for you to do. Most of these buildings haven't been cleaned out and organized in a while and I don't have time to do it."

"I love organizing things," Olivia said.

"I'm in the middle of a couple of projects right

now. Give me until tomorrow morning and I'll set you up with something."

"Sure." She could feel her spirits lifting already. "Thanks." This was a good idea. Coming to Painted Rock was a good idea.

He brushed his hands together to wipe off the straw and dust. "Enjoy your day off."

Olivia relaxed into a genuine smile as she walked out of the corral, through a maze of gleaming white fences and across a section of pasture. Chin up, shoulders back, she was finally feeling like her old self.

Arms swinging at her sides, she ploughed up a nearby grassy hill toward the tree line. There was one particular pine she'd spotted from Claudia's back door. A big one with a wide, lacey-looking shadow underneath it. It would be an easy hike up there and she could get a good view of Claudia's ranch.

The view was as gorgeous as she'd imagined. She could see a good chunk of the ranch and even a little bit of downtown Painted Rock.

A little farther up the hill, into the thicker part of the forest, a rocky shelf jutted out of the earth. If she stood up there she'd get an even better view of the town. She headed toward it, soaking up the sun and enjoying just being outside.

She was nearly there when she heard a cracking sound. Then another.

No, not a crack. A rifle shot.

Ice water swirled through her veins. She spun around, but she didn't know what she was looking for. Which direction had the sounds come from?

Her pulse hammered furiously and it was hard to take a breath. She tried to tell herself that in a wilderness area, gunfire wasn't a big deal. People probably shot at things all the time. Rattlesnakes. Mountain lions. Rabid coyotes. No one was targeting her. She was overreacting.

Then she heard another shot. This one was closer. Something tugged at the shoulder of her shirt. She looked down and immediately wished she hadn't.

Blood. Sprayed like a fine red mist across the stones. She put her hand to her shoulder and pulled it away. More blood. *Her* blood.

FOUR

Olivia's legs felt as heavy and unwieldly as bags of wet cement. Dizziness sent her vision spiraling in such nauseating waves she thought she might be sick.

Her injured shoulder burned like fire, but the arm below it felt strangely numb and useless. Blind panic propelled her forward. She didn't have a destination. She just flung herself onward, driven by terror. *He's trying to kill me.*

Another shot cracked through the silence. From a different direction this time, but she couldn't think where. Behind? In front?

She clambered over the rocky hillside as best she could, between pine trees and over tall, yellowing grass. She stumbled over the stone shelves jutting up from the ground, narrowly avoiding a face-plant.

Which direction had the shot come from? What if she was moving toward the shooter?

She tried to clear her mind, but her senses

were abandoning her. Except for her vision. That was improving as the swirling dizziness slowed and finally stopped.

At that point a dormant part of her brain woke up. A part that told her she was smarter and wilier than she thought herself to be. *Look! Use your eyes! Find a place to hide!*

She'd received safety training for her job at the shelter, but that focused on urban situations. Most of it didn't apply here. Disoriented, she had no idea which way to run for help. Trees, rock outcroppings and tall grass surrounded her. A few minutes ago they had been beautiful but now they were terrifying. Any one of them could be hiding the shooter.

Claudia's house was downhill, but downhill *which way?*

Think! If she kept stumbling around, the shooter was sure to find her. She was acting like panicked, witless prey. But that was not the true Olivia Dillon. *It was not.*

She slid to a stop, ignoring the way her heart hammered. In the quiet stillness between her own raspy gasps for air she heard a snap.

Not a gunshot. Something else. Coming closer.

"Oh, God, help me."

The sound of her own desperate, whispered cry brought a fresh round of tears to her eyes. Her gaze lit on a rock shelf with a pair of short, slender pine trees in front of it. The hollow between the flat slab of stone and the dirt beneath wasn't very big, but maybe she could lie down and slide in. It might be full of snakes but they'd just have to get out of her way. She was *not* going to just stand there and get shot. She was *not* going to give up and collapse in terror. Not this time.

She dropped down and crawled forward toward the mouth of the opening, forcing her numb arm to do its share of work despite the searing pain in her shoulder. She refused to look behind her. If the shooter was there, she was already trapped. If that was the case, she didn't want to know.

As she crawled forward, her hand slid across a long, narrow tree branch that had fallen to the ground. She wrapped her fingers around the branch and held on tight. Inching forward, she reached the opening beneath the rock shelf and jabbed the tree branch into it. She braced herself for a snake's venom-tipped strike—but it didn't happen.

Gritting her teeth, she reached forward, pushing aside the young pines in front of the opening and crawling into the small void formed between the rock and the dirt. She pulled her feet in last and let the limber young trees bend back into place to partly conceal her hiding place.

There was barely enough room for her to turn her head to face the opening. She breathed in dirt, tasting its metallic tang on her tongue. Her exhalations stirred up a small cloud of soil and tiny bits of decaying plants. The dusty mess stuck to the sweat on her neck and to the blood on her shoulder and arm.

She tried to hold her breath and listen, but her body seemed starved for oxygen and she couldn't stop panting. From where she lay she couldn't see much of anything outside her little cave. But after a few minutes she heard something. It sounded like someone walking. Then the footsteps stopped.

Moving very slowly, she lifted her head and saw a man walk by, carrying a rifle and wearing a knitted black ski mask. Was it Ted Kurtz? She couldn't tell.

A cold chill shot through her body and she started to feel dizzy again. She had to drop her head back down and concentrate on staying conscious. A few deep breaths, a few seconds of willing her mind to stay focused, and her thoughts finally cleared.

Was the man with the rifle still out there? Had he wandered off, still looking for her? While fighting the wave of dizziness, she'd lost track of where he was. She was afraid to try to lift herself up and look back outside again.

The hiding place she'd been so happy to find suddenly seemed too tight and confining. Too much like a grave. Her panting breaths turned to shallow gasps. She thought she might be hyperventilating.

What if she passed out? Even if Claudia had heard the rifle shots and sent someone to look for her, they might not ever find her if she stayed in this hole in the ground.

Straining to listen, she heard only the breeze rustling the pine branches. Then she heard a voice. A man's voice. She held her breath and listened very hard. It sounded as if he was calling her name.

"Olivia! Are you out here? It's me, Elijah. It's okay. I'm going to help you."

"Here!" Olivia tried to call out. "I'm here!" But the sound she made wasn't very loud.

She tried a second time, straining to make her voice louder, but her body wouldn't cooperate. Her thoughts started turning woozy again and she felt cold.

She reached for a branch on one of the little pine trees at the opening of her hiding place and tugged it, hoping the rustling would draw Elijah's attention. The tree barely moved. She gritted her teeth and put every ounce of her strength into tugging it again.

Suddenly Elijah's hand was clasping hers. Tears of relief flooded her eyes.

He dropped down so that he was looking at her from just a few inches away. "Hey, what are you doing in there?" he asked in a gentle voice so at odds with his usual tough, unsmiling expression. Even now, he didn't offer her a smile. He just looked at her with a world of tender compassion in those obsidian eyes and said, "Let me get you out of there."

She held out her other hand, the one covered with blood and dirt. He took hold of it without hesitation and helped her out.

"What happened to you?"

"Sh-shot." A chill shook her body, but at least her voice was back. "My sh-shoulder."

"Yeah, I heard it. I was afraid it was you." He started at the top of her head and quickly patted down her body. "Let me see if you got nicked anywhere else," he said. "I've been shot and didn't know it until later."

"How could you not know?"

He got out his phone and dialed 911, asking for EMS to meet him at Claudia's, and quickly explaining what had happened. He was so calm and cool that Olivia started to get angry. She'd been *shot*. He'd found her bleeding and hiding in a hole in the ground. Shouldn't he be freaking out a little bit? Didn't she deserve that?

He helped her to her feet, and then peeled off the light flannel shirt he was wearing over a T-shirt and wrapped the flannel around her. Then he tucked his arm around her shoulder and they started down the hill in a direction that didn't look at all familiar.

She had to be in shock because she was on the verge of laughing. But then, almost as quickly, she was on the verge of tears again. She had been *shot*. She could have died.

Feeling insignificant in a cold, hard universe, she stumbled down the hillside until they reached Elijah's motorcycle.

He helped her onto the seat, sat down behind her and cranked up the engine.

"What kind of cowboy are you?" Olivia muttered. "Why don't you have a horse?"

"I do have a horse." He pulled her back so she rested against him. She melted into his muscled chest, soaking up his strength and feeling safe for the first time in a long while.

"The sheriff's department will need help searching the countryside for any sign of Kurtz. After I get you to the hospital, I'll go home, saddle up my horse Churchill and ride back over here. If Ted Kurtz is out here, we'll find him."

"No!" Fear shot through Olivia. She gripped his shirt and shook her head. "I don't want him to shoot you, too."

"It's okay." He brought his arms closer together, held her a little tighter and revved the engine. "I'm not the one you need to worry about."

After making sure Olivia was safely transported to the hospital, Elijah joined the other volunteers who'd gathered near the shooting site and started combing the hillside, looking for any clues left behind by the shooter. Five hours later, he was still looking.

"Elijah! Hold up!"

He turned his buckskin in the direction of the voice. Churchill was so sure-footed he practically moved like a cat. "What did you find?" Elijah demanded, as Jonathan rode up.

Jonathan, Elijah's younger brother, was also searching the ridge between Claudia's ranch and the Morales ranch. Deputy Bedford rode beside him. Discovering the deputy rode had improved Elijah's opinion of him.

"Nobody's seen anything since you found the bullet casings and those footprints," Jonathan said. The footprints had led to a rocky stretch of land that went on for miles. Elijah had been riding at the edge of the rock outcropping for hours, trying to pick up the shooter's trail.

"Sheriff Wolfsinger is wrapping up the search." Jonathan rubbed the newly grown tuft of hair below his bottom lip. A "soul patch" he called it. Apparently to a nineteen-year-old it looked cool. Elijah thought it looked ridiculous.

"The sheriff says it's getting too dark," Jonathan added.

"It's not dark yet."

"I told him you'd say that."

"We might as well stop," Bedford said. "Everybody's just riding over each other's tracks at this point."

Elijah's phone rang and Claudia's name came up on the screen. Last he'd heard from her, she was at the hospital with Olivia.

"How are you?" Claudia asked when he answered.

"How are *you*? You've been at the hospital all day. You must be tired. I'll have Jonathan pick you up and drive you home."

"You mother's coming to get me in a little bit."

"Good. How's your niece?"

"She's doing well. Doc Beamer was able to get her shoulder sewed up. No serious injuries, no fractures, nothing like that."

"Glad to hear it." And relieved. Seeing her bleeding and shaking had worried him. She hadn't looked particularly healthy even before she got shot.

"They were going to discharge her, but the doctor changed his mind at the last minute. He thinks she should stay overnight. She's pretty run-down."

He heard Olivia say something in the background, but he couldn't make out the words.

"It's for the best, honey," he heard Claudia say. For the next few seconds the two women argued. Both sounded polite, though he could tell by Olivia's tone she wasn't very happy. He didn't envy Claudia having to be with Olivia at that moment.

Then again, maybe he did. A little. Just because there was something fascinating about Olivia Dillon. Even when she was cranky. Which, as far as he could tell, was all the time. She wasn't insulting or cruel. She'd just been rubbed a little raw by life lately, and Elijah could relate to that.

"So, yes, Olivia's okay," Claudia said to Elijah, directing her conversation back to him. "Are you finished up there on the ridge?"

"Almost."

"Well, you be careful."

"You, too." Elijah disconnected and slid the phone back into his pocket. He reached down to give Churchill a couple of pats on his neck while looking around at the nearby hills and the purple mesas in the distance. "I hate to leave without figuring out how that shooter got up here and back out again."

"He must have hiked or driven along a main road, then crossed Aunt Claudia's land or ours," Jonathan said. Elijah frowned at him. If it were true, whoever was hunting Olivia was skilled and stealthy.

"I don't want to believe it, either." Jonathan glanced around. "But there's no other explanation. Unless he rode a horse or a bike to the back-country and hiked down here."

"That doesn't sound like the fat-cat lawyer Miss Dillon's worried about," Bedford muttered. "Sounds more like hired firepower."

If that was true, Olivia was especially fortunate she'd survived. Elijah glanced upward. *Thank You, Lord.*

"Anyone trying to help Miss Dillon might be crossing some very dangerous people," Bedford said to Elijah. "I know about your military service, and I'm not saying you can't handle yourself. But this might require more extensive resources and backup than you've got. You don't want to hunt this guy on your own."

Elijah wasn't exactly on his own. But he wouldn't ask his friends in Vanquish the Darkness to put themselves in harm's way. They were organized to provide spiritual comfort, particularly for veterans and their families, and to reach out to people in hospitals and other facilities who might have been otherwise forgotten. The riders had crossed paths with a few unsavory people along the way—it couldn't be avoided—but they weren't some personal protection group under Elijah's direction.

"How well do you know Olivia Dillon, anyway?" Bedford asked.

"I just met her last night."

"Why such a personal interest?"

Elijah shrugged. He didn't want to talk about it.

"Mrs. Somerset," Jonathan said quietly.

Bedford glanced at Jonathan and then back at Elijah as though expecting an explanation. He wasn't going to get one. Mrs. Somerset was only one name on the long list of war casualties Elijah knew personally. In her case, she was a woman he should have protected but didn't.

Jonathan knew the whole ugly story, yet the kid still looked up to his big brother. Sometimes his admiration made Elijah feel like a fraud.

"We just going to sit around here?" Elijah said gruffly, aware he'd started to drift into the past again. "If we move out, form a wide perimeter and look closely one more time, maybe we can find some tracks or trampled grass we missed earlier before we call it a night."

"Worth a try," Bedford agreed.

Jonathan nodded. "Let's do it."

They rode until full dark, staying in contact

by phone, but found nothing. "If I hear anything I'm authorized to tell you, I'll let you know," Bedford promised.

When he got home, Elijah cooled down Churchill and made sure he was fed and watered. Then he got in his truck, drove to the hospital and found Olivia's room.

Olivia lay in bed, sleeping. With her bruises and bandages, she looked as if she'd gone a few rounds with a prizefighter. In a way, she had.

She needed somebody to look after her, whether she wanted to admit it or not.

Elijah dropped his tired body into a chair at the foot of her bed to keep watch.

FIVE

Olivia opened her eyes. In the pale blue early-morning light she saw Elijah slumped in a chair in her hospital room. In weathered jeans, a black T-shirt, a jean jacket and heavy black motorcycle boots, he looked out of place with the pale fuchsia wall behind him holding a framed print of two white poodle puppies chasing a butterfly.

The last time she'd woken, Claudia had been sitting in that chair. Before that, Olivia had opened her eyes to a nurse in recovery asking her silly questions about the current month, the time of the year and how many eggs were in a dozen. And before that, she remembered a doctor telling her that she might end up with an impressive scar on her upper arm, but otherwise she would be okay. Time seemed to be moving both backward and forward.

"Hey," Olivia called out.

Elijah stirred and lifted his head. He must be

a light sleeper. Olivia's voice hadn't come out much louder than a whisper.

"Hey," he answered back, sitting up and rubbing his eyes with the heels of his hands.

"Sleeping in that chair will give you a stiff neck."

"I can sleep anywhere." He had an appealing scruff of beard going. He rubbed a hand over it and through his bristly black hair before standing up and walking toward her bed.

"How are you feeling?"

She glanced at her bandaged shoulder and back at him. "Right now? No pain." The pain medicine was still in her body, making her feel as if she was wrapped in a cocoon. "But I have a feeling it's going to sting when the medicine wears off."

"Only when you laugh."

She laughed. And as her laugh died out, the memory of what had happened came rushing back. Along with the feelings of sheer terror and hopelessness. She was still shaken by the unnerving realization that someone had actually shot her. Had tried to *kill* her. She felt her eyes tear up and her face begin to crumple.

"We didn't get him," Elijah said, standing at her bedside, hands crossed in front of his body, eyes downcast as though it was his personal responsibility to catch Kurtz.

Olivia drew in a ragged breath. For a few seconds she'd felt safe, her worries vague and half-forgotten. Too bad it hadn't lasted a little longer.

She reached out for his hand and managed to grasp the tips of his fingers. "Hey. Thanks for rescuing me. Again."

His gaze met hers. "From what I saw, it looked like you rescued yourself. I just got there for the mop-up."

Coming from someone who didn't appear to smile unless he felt like it, who couldn't or wouldn't turn on the easy, facile charm that so many people used to get through life, his words meant something. And he was right. She had managed to keep herself from getting killed. Even in the grip of stark terror she wasn't helpless. She hadn't collapsed into a whimpering heap and given up.

She squeezed his fingers. "Nevertheless, thank you."

He nodded and seemed about to say something when a big bouquet of flowers suddenly filled the space behind him and a voice sang out, "You're awake!"

Claudia stepped around Elijah, hefting a round white basket full of purple irises and yellow roses. She glanced at him. "I had a feeling you'd be here." She set the basket on a table beside Olivia's bed. "Honey, how are you?"

Olivia relaxed into a slight smile. It had been a long time since anybody fussed over her. "I don't feel so bad."

"Good." Claudia sat down on the edge of her bed.

"But I'd like to get out of here as soon as I can."

"I'll drive you," Elijah said. "Just in case."

"The doctor said he wanted to talk to you after you woke up and ate some breakfast." Claudia's upbeat tone sounded forced. "If everything looks good, he'll send you home."

Home. Where *was* that, exactly? Not Las Vegas anymore. Not anywhere. Again, in an instant, Olivia's spirits crashed. Hopefully, her seesawing emotions were a result of the medicine and not a new way of life. She'd counseled women who'd been shot at when she was working at the safe house, interning on her way to becoming a social worker. She'd learned basic counseling skills, but at the moment she couldn't remember any of the advice she'd been trained to give to someone who'd survived a physical attack.

"I called your mom and dad. Each of them said they'd call you sometime today. And both of them said to let them know if you need anything."

How sweet. Some parents might actually rush to visit their daughter after she'd been shot.

"How come our family didn't spend any time together when I was growing up?" Olivia asked. "Why didn't we visit you, or any of my other relatives, when I was a kid? Why didn't we spend Christmases together?"

Claudia's smile faded. "Honey, if there was some reason, some feud going on, I don't know anything about it. I think everybody got busy. Time passed and we all settled into routines that didn't involve each other. We came to visit you once, do you remember?"

"Yes."

"It was always hard to get Hugh away from the ranch. He worried about the animals. Not the horses or the stock animals. We had help with them. He worried about the cats and the dogs. And his birds and his bunnies. We invited your parents to come out but they never could make it." Claudia shrugged. "I guess, like anything else, relationships can die from neglect."

"But not our newfound relationship," Olivia said firmly.

"No, not ours."

Okay, enough of that. Olivia sniffed and brushed her hair out of her eyes with her good hand, determined not to think about things that would only send her spirits crashing again. Instead, she'd think about how Elijah had gone looking for her after he heard gunshots. He'd helped her down the hill. Claudia had opened her home to her and was right now sitting in front of her. That was more than a lot of people had.

She glanced around for Elijah just as a uniformed hospital security officer walked by the open door, paused to look in, waved and then continued down the hallway.

Claudia followed her gaze. "You looking for Elijah? He slipped out a minute ago. I hope he went home to get some sleep. He spent hours with the sheriff's department and some local search-and-tracking volunteers trying to find the man who did this to you."

"There's so much wilderness around here. I'd think it would be impossible to find someone intent on hiding."

"They had to stop looking when it got dark. That's when Elijah came here to the hospital. He stayed all night."

It wasn't anything personal, Olivia told herself. She needed to get a few things straight in her head before she started to believe he felt a deeper concern for her. Elijah Morales might look rugged and he might even be rugged, but he was a church guy. Helping people was what church guys did. They'd do it for anybody.

Again, the tears started. Olivia was beginning to think she'd never be able to completely turn them off again. She couldn't help it. The truth was, deep in her heart, she wanted to be very important to somebody.

"I'm so sorry." Claudia reached for Olivia's hand. Tears began to form in the corners of her eyes, too.

"Don't cry, Aunt Claudia. You have nothing to be sorry for."

"Yes I do," she answered forcefully. "I told you to get outside and go for a walk." Her voice cracked. "I told you it was safe."

"And I let myself get careless."

As she watched Claudia dab at her eyes with a tissue, Olivia felt a flash of emotion. Something familiar, like a fleeting glimpse of her former self. It put some strength into her spine. "We're *not* going to do this," she said, reaching for the hem of Claudia's bright yellow blouse and tugging on it until her aunt finally looked at her. "We are *not* going to blame ourselves."

Claudia nodded and Olivia smiled at her. She hadn't thought of herself as a strong woman for a while. Not since the debacle with Kurtz started. But she was still alive. She was a survivor.

Elijah picked up Olivia at the hospital and got her into his truck as quickly as he could. Since the shooter hadn't been caught, he wanted her safe in his family's house. And Claudia would be safer traveling in a separate vehicle. Fortunately, Claudia agreed with his plan and helped talk Olivia into it. Claudia had called him as soon as the doctor signed Olivia's release forms.

"Are you sure your family's okay with me going to your house?" Olivia asked, running the hand from her uninjured arm through her hair as she fidgeted nervously in the passenger seat of his truck. Claudia followed along in her own car as they pulled out of the hospital parking lot. "The last thing I want to do is put somebody else in danger."

"My parents love company," Elijah answered. "And they're used to trouble."

Most of it brought by him.

He stopped at a red light on Stagecoach Road, in what passed for downtown Painted Rock, and then turned left toward the Morales ranch.

"Aunt Claudia's fortunate to have your family living so close by," Olivia said.

Elijah glanced over and saw her looking at all the small downtown businesses.

"Wide-open space can be nice. But being isolated gets old. It's good to have neighbors." In the side mirror jutting out from the truck he could see Claudia following along in her pearl-white sedan.

Elijah looked ahead, then right and left before he moved forward when the light changed. Kurtz or a hired gun could be anywhere. He kept an eye on the vehicles nearby, trying to make sure no one other than Claudia was following them.

"There might be some riders hanging around the house," he said. "I know you won't remember them from the night you came into town, but a couple of them remember you. And they want to help."

He glanced over to see her reaction. Some people were uncomfortable with motorcycle riders. If that was the case with Olivia, he'd need to come up with another plan.

"Vanquish the Darkness. That's a pretty dramatic name for a group." She didn't sound as if the idea of them being around bothered her.

"The founders wanted a name that made a statement."

"It certainly does that."

In his peripheral vision he saw her studying him. He was thankful for his dark sunglasses. When she took his hand and looked into his eyes to thank him this morning, it felt as if she was looking right into him. It was unnerving. It must have been because he was tired. He hadn't really slept in that chair, just dozed a little.

"Do you just stare ahead with that stony expression all the time?" Olivia asked.

Elijah made another turn at the next light. "I guess so." This was already starting to get uncomfortably personal.

"Relax," she said a few seconds later. "We're not on a date or anything."

"No, we aren't." Elijah didn't date.

"I'm not your type. I'm sure you're way too noble to tell a huge lie like I did. And you'd never drag danger to *your* great-aunt's doorstep."

Her quiet anger had sprung from nowhere. Elijah glanced over to make sure she was okay. She sat rigidly, her body radiating tension. He hadn't done anything but drive since they got into his truck, so she couldn't be mad at him. It sounded like she was mad at herself.

Her comment did remind him of the sad reality that she hadn't had a thing to do with Claudia until she'd needed her aunt's help. Olivia might be an intriguing woman, but she was also an unknown. Right now, she was an unknown with danger swirling all around her. Time to remember to use his brain and leave his emotions at the door.

They drove on in silence for several minutes until Olivia relaxed back into her seat, head against the headrest, the fight having apparently drained out of her. She blew out a loud breath. "Hey, thanks for the great conversation."

He laughed. She didn't join in with him this time.

A huge pine beam with the name Morales burned into it rested atop two parallel beams and formed the arched entrance to the Morales family ranch. Elijah turned into it, heading down the dusty, winding drive.

"So this is where your motorcycle gang hides out?" Olivia asked. "What's the story?"

"This isn't a hideout. It's my family's home. If you're asking about Vanquish, the short answer is that people who liked to ride and wanted to band together to be of service started it years ago. My parents were involved. Over the years it died off. It was recently restarted by me."

Well, be careful when you want to help people. Things can turn ugly."

Elijah already knew that. It didn't stop him from helping. He turned to her. "Do you ride?"

"No. I hate motorcycles."

"Have you ever actually ridden one?"

"Other than yesterday? No. Still, I've never actually inhaled a lamb chop but I know I don't want to do that, either."

He chuckled a little and felt the tension in his shoulders relax. At least he didn't have to guess what she was thinking. The woman said exactly what was on her mind.

"You were in the military," she said. It was a statement rather than a question. "I knew it the first time I saw you."

"United States Army Ranger."

"Were you in Iraq or Afghanistan?"

"Both."

From the corner of his eye he saw her look down at her hands in her lap.

"That had to be a life-altering experience." She sighed. "I appreciate your service, but I'm sorry you had to go through it. I don't know what else to say."

"You don't have to say anything."

"Maybe you're right," she said a few minutes later. "With that combat experience I don't need to worry about you. Ted Kurtz is the one who should be worried."

Elijah felt a smile tug at the corner of his lips. He parked his truck. "I hope you like chili verde. Mom's had it simmering all day. The smell's got to be making Dad crazy by now. He loves the stuff."

Olivia fumbled for the door handle. Elijah came around the truck, opened the door for her and helped her out.

Behind them, Claudia had already gotten out of her car.

"Hey, Aunt Claudia," Elijah's mom called out.

Claudia walked by them, giving Olivia a light pat as she passed by, and then continuing up the steps to greet Julie Morales with a hug.

"Your mom's pretty," Olivia said. "She doesn't look a thing like you."

"Good thing for her." Elijah quickly gathered up Olivia's hospital paperwork and prescriptions from the front seat. He was trying to appear calm. The reality was that he was worried. The shooter had managed to come down from the backcountry yesterday without attracting anyone's attention and without leaving a readable trail.

"Welcome to the casa," Elijah said, gesturing up the steps to the house.

"Olivia, honey, come meet Julie." Claudia waved Olivia over when she reached the porch.

Olivia offered Julie a shy smile.

"Welcome to our home." The slight breeze buffeted her long mahogany hair. She had a fluid, free-spirited air about her appearance and movements. In that respect Elijah was nothing like his mom.

"Your aunt told us about you as soon as she found out you were coming for a visit." Julie glanced at Claudia and they shared a smile. "I'm so sorry about what's happened since your arrival." Her smile faded as she looked at Olivia's injured shoulder.

"Speaking of that, let's get inside." Elijah looked around at the trees and buildings on the property. There were all kinds of places where a shooter could hide.

"Thanks for welcoming me into your home," Olivia said to Julie as Elijah ushered the ladies inside. "I used to work in a safe house. I never dreamed one day I would need one."

SIX

The first thing Olivia noticed in the Morales home was the delicious aroma. The smell of simmering chili verde was rich and comforting. The second thing she noticed was how different the interior was from Claudia's fussy, lacy home.

She stepped through the front door onto a cobalt-blue-and-sunflower-yellow-patterned tile floor. A few feet out, steps led down to a thickly carpeted living room with two oxblood-colored leather sofas positioned opposite each other. Oversize chairs and low, heavy tables were positioned around the room. There was also a massive stone fireplace.

Directly in front of her, three tinted picture windows offered views of a wide veranda attached to the house, and hills and ranch buildings in the distance.

"Don't worry," Elijah said from beside her. "We tinted the larger windows to prevent any bad guys from taking an easy shot at us while we're inside the house. Mom still wanted curtains because she thinks they make the house feel cozier. If the shooter's out there, he can't see in."

"Thanks for that," Olivia muttered.

He gave her a questioning look.

"For a few seconds there, I almost forgot my troubles."

"I hope you don't mind eating buffet-style," Julie called out from the kitchen.

With Elijah gesturing for her to walk ahead of him, Olivia followed the voice to a kitchen with a breakfast nook at one end. Windows showed more of the ranch, including several motorcycles parked outside.

Claudia was already in the kitchen. So were three other people Olivia hadn't seen before.

"We can't always eat at the same time around here," Julie said, "so I'm in the habit of cooking something and then letting everybody plate it up themselves. Usually we eat in the living room. It's good to sink down onto a sofa and put your feet up at the end of the day. It might not be the most proper way to have dinner, but it's our way."

"Sounds wonderful to me." Smelled wonderful, too.

Julie gave the pot one more stir, and then turned to Olivia with a smile. Which immediately turned to a frown. "Oh dear, what was I thinking?" She looked pointedly at Olivia's injured shoulder and her arm immobilized in a sling.

"I'll help her," Elijah said.

"I can manage." Olivia was beginning to feel like a stray cat Elijah had fed and now he was stuck with her.

"Well, as you can see there's shredded cheese, chopped cilantro, sour cream and a few other things here on the counter." Julie had already turned her attention back to the food. "And I've got some warm corn and flour tortillas."

"Just let me know what you want," Elijah said to Olivia. "You go sit in the living room and I'll bring it to you."

She wanted to tell him where *he* could go sit. "It's not your job to look after me," she whispered back. Protecting her from danger was one thing, but hovering over her all the time was another. She wasn't used to anyone working so hard to take care of her, and it left her edgy and unsure how to respond.

He was acting like a boyfriend and she didn't need that. Not now, when her emotions were so raw. If she let him keep it up, she would get confused. She would start to think his behavior meant something it obviously didn't. And she didn't want to get involved with him, anyway.

Who wanted a relationship with the town hero who looked like a scowling statue half the time?

"Olivia?"

Olivia's head snapped up. She was tired and without realizing it her gaze had settled on the kitchen floor.

"Let me introduce you to some of our rider friends before we start eating," Julie said.

"Riders who are part of Vanquish the Darkness?"

Julie nodded. "This is Bobby."

A young man who couldn't be much more than twenty, sporting curly red hair and neon-blue half-glasses, smiled and nodded.

"He's our techie," Elijah said quietly. "Anybody has computer or phone issues, we rely on him."

"And this fine couple would be Mark and Linda."

Julie gestured toward a lanky man with thinning hair who looked to be about Elijah's age. "Mark's a cowboy. He works here at the ranch. Linda is a juvenile probation officer."

Linda was a petite blonde woman barely more than half her husband's height.

"There are women riders in Vanquish?" Olivia asked.

Linda smiled broadly and nodded. "Absolutely."

"Let's see," Julie continued. "Have you met

my son Jonathan?" she asked as a tall, slender young man with a shy smile walked around a corner and into the kitchen. "Where's—oh, there you are," she said as a dark-haired, bronze-skinned man came around the corner. "Honey, meet Olivia Dillon. Olivia, this is my husband, Joe."

"Welcome," Joe said.

A man of few words, like his son.

Olivia took a deep breath and positioned herself so she was facing everyone. "If you don't already know, you'll know soon enough that I told a lie that almost sent a man to prison." She looked around the room. "Everybody should know that before you sign on to help me. And if you want to back out, I don't blame you."

"We've all made mistakes." Joe glanced around the kitchen and everyone nodded. He turned to Olivia. "Our offer of help isn't just for perfect people." He clapped his hands together and smiled. "Now, let's give thanks for the food and dig in!"

After they prayed, Julie made sure Elijah started a plate for Olivia.

"Why don't you go sit down," Claudia whispered in Olivia's ear. "You must be tired."

"I am."

Olivia found a spot on one of the couches in the living room. Elijah pulled a coffee table close

in front of her, set down her food and some cut-
lery, and then came back with a glass of iced tea
and a cloth napkin.

When he came back with his own dinner, he
sat as far away from her as possible. He immediately engrossed himself in talking with Bobby
and his brother.

She got the message.

And yet, there was a moment after he'd
walked with her down from the ridge, when they
were on his motorcycle, when he was getting her
settled and then taking off to meet up with the
ambulance at Claudia's house, when she'd felt
a connection with him. And she'd thought he'd
felt it, too. He'd held her close and she'd felt his
strength radiating into her. She'd needed him
and he'd been there. She'd poured all her trust
into him without a second thought and he'd safe-
guarded it. And her. She was sure they'd shared
some kind of bond.

She must have been delusional from loss of
blood.

When she finished eating, Olivia set her
empty plate on the low table in front of her.
"Thank you, that was delicious."

Julie smiled, "Glad you liked it."

Joe, who sat beside her, patted his wife's knee.
"I'm a lucky man." From what Olivia could see
he laughed and smiled easily, unlike his son.

"Okay," Elijah said briskly. "We need a plan on how we're going to keep an eye on Olivia and find out who's after her."

"Aunt Claudia, I could get a security system up around your house that would cover all the main buildings." Bobby pushed his neon-blue glasses up his nose while looking at an electronic tablet balanced on his lap. "You could monitor it from your kitchen or your bedroom or wherever you want."

He glanced up for a response. Claudia, who was sitting on the couch beside Olivia, looked at him for a long time before slowly shaking her head. "I don't know if I could live like that. Feeling like I'm always under observation." She glanced at Olivia. "I know it's the way of the world these days. But it's not the way for me."

"I don't want you to have to change your lifestyle," Olivia said.

"It wouldn't have to be permanent." Bobby glanced back and forth between Claudia and Elijah.

"No," Olivia said a little more forcefully. "If she doesn't want to do it, she doesn't have to."

"You're right, of course," Joe said calmly. "No one's going to force anyone to do anything." He glanced at Bobby. "It's a good idea, but we'll just have to think of something else."

Olivia's faced burned with regret. "I'm sorry."

She shook her head and cleared her throat. "I appreciate your help. Everybody's help. I don't know what I would have done without you." Her gaze drifted to Elijah. His dark eyes were focused on her, but he kept hidden whatever emotion might lie behind them. Then she turned to Claudia. "I thought I could leave whatever danger was trailing me back in Las Vegas. I didn't mean to bring it here."

"It's not your fault," Joe said.

How many times had Olivia sat across from a woman at the safe house and uttered those same words? They were so much easier to believe when you were the one saying them. Harder to believe when you were on the receiving end.

"Olivia, honey, I was so happy when you called and said you'd decided to come visit that I couldn't fall asleep that night," Claudia said, her voice a little shaky. "I'm still glad you came."

"We don't have to decide everything right now," Elijah said. "But it would be a good idea for you to spend tonight in a place where you'll have plenty of people looking out for you."

"Spend the night?"

Julie caught her eye and said gently, "I bet right now you really want to get some rest."

It was true. She was exhausted, and her arm and shoulder ached. Elijah had grabbed her pain pills from the car, but she didn't know where he'd put them and she hated to ask someone to go get them.

"Do you really think Kurtz might try to shoot me again?" She directed her question at Elijah.

He shrugged. "What was your experience when you worked at the safe house? Could you predict what anybody would do?"

"No." She let go a sigh. "When someone's mind is twisted and angry, they're capable of anything."

"Yeah." His expression softened slightly and she could see compassion in his eyes. "That's been my experience, too."

A few minutes later, Elijah walked into the house from the back veranda, disconnecting from his call and tucking his phone into his back pocket. Everyone in the family room looked up at him. "Deputy Bedford will be by in the morning." He turned to Olivia. "He wants to talk to you again."

She nodded and looked down, seeming to shrink in upon herself as if she was trying to disappear. He wanted to go over and sit next to her, put an arm around her, tell her he would make sure nothing bad happened to her. But that would not be a good idea.

Having other members of Vanquish around reminded him that he hadn't revived the church's motorcycle outreach group to find himself a girl-friend. He'd done it because there were so many people who needed help. And because he'd sur-vived so much when others hadn't. He had a debt to pay.

"Has Bedford developed any leads?" Mark asked.

"Nothing he was willing to talk about over the phone."

"I think I'd like to lie down," Olivia said qui-etly. She turned to Claudia. "How about you?"

Claudia nodded.

"Are we sharing a room?" Olivia asked.

Claudia glanced at her niece, and then looked away. Apparently she hadn't told Olivia they'd agreed that only she would stay the night.

Elijah stepped in to fill the awkward silence. It had been his idea, anyway. "We thought it would be good if you stayed here tonight." He glanced at Claudia and she gave him an uncer-tain smile. "But your aunt wants to go home and sleep in her own bed."

"I can't sleep anywhere else," she said apolo-getically.

"And I can't imagine you got much sleep last night," Julie threw in. "Not after everything that happened."

"No." Claudia shook her head. "I didn't." She

turned to Olivia. "Also I really need to get home to feed the dogs and the cats."

"Raymond and Denise don't take care of the animals?"

"No."

"Oh." Olivia bit her bottom lip and rubbed her injured arm.

"Is your pain medication wearing off?" Elijah asked.

"I don't know." She sounded disoriented. Then she nodded. "Yeah, I think so."

"Let me get it for you." He headed for the kitchen.

He read the directions on the sheet of paper the hospital had given Olivia, filled a glass of water, took a pill out of a bottle, and jotted down the time and dosage on the back of the paper.

He walked back into the living room and held out the pill and the water.

She wouldn't look him in the eye, but she took the medicine. When she reached out to take the pill from his hand, her skin felt warm. He hoped she wasn't getting a fever. Her body had been through a lot in the past thirty or so hours. *She* had been through a lot.

"I hope this pill doesn't make me groggy in the morning," Olivia said wearily.

"According to the directions, I don't think it'll last more than six hours."

"Good. I've got a job interview tomorrow."

"Are you sure?" It was the first Elijah had heard of it. Maybe Olivia was confused. Maybe the drugs from the hospital combined with the pain and the terror she'd been through were mixing her up.

"At the senior living facility. Golden Sands." Elijah turned to Claudia and she nodded.

"Aunt Claudia knows the guy that runs the place," Olivia added. "They need somebody to help with their arts-and-crafts program. It's just part-time, but it's something."

She was beginning to sniffle, as if she might cry. Her reddish-blond hair had fallen in front of her eyes and Elijah was so tempted to reach out and brush it away that he made himself take a step back. He needed to keep his eyes and ears open. Stay objective. Avoid getting emotionally involved. She'd be safer that way.

"You should reschedule the interview," he said.

"No!" This time she did look at him, her eyes glistening with unshed tears. But her expression wasn't sad. Or pleading. She was clearly determined.

She sniffed loudly and sat up straighter. "I lost my job in Las Vegas and I've had a hard time finding another one. This wouldn't be the same kind of work that I was doing, but it would be meaningful. Aunt Claudia lined up the opportunity for me and I intend to make the best of it."

She turned to Elijah. "So, no. I won't reschedule. I'm going."

"Okay," Elijah said. "I'll take you."

"Thank you." Olivia used her good arm to push herself up off the couch. "I'm going back to the house with you," she said to Claudia. "After everything that's happened, I don't think you should go back alone."

"She won't," Linda said brightly, also standing up. "Mark and I are going with her." She beamed at Claudia. "I love that cute little office with the day bed you have downstairs by the kitchen. And Mark's never met a couch that didn't double as the perfect bed for him. He'll sleep in the living room."

Olivia's jaw dropped slightly as she looked around the room. Her gaze finally settled on Elijah.

"Well, you've certainly got all this planned, don't you?" she said.

"It's what we do."

She turned to Claudia "After everything that's happened, you and I should stick together. I could go back to your house with you. Elijah could come, too. We'd have three people protecting us."

"You and I can move into Claudia's house tomorrow," Elijah said.

"Why wait?"

"Because nobody's out to kill your eighty-year-old aunt. They're after you. If Kurtz is that determined, he may try something tonight, when he knows you're already injured and vulnerable. I would think you wouldn't want Aunt Claudia in the same house with you. *I* don't want her in the same house with you. We'll have time tomorrow to make her house more secure before you move back in."

"Oh. That makes sense." The fire went out of her eyes.

Elijah turned to Mark and Linda. "Now that we've got that settled, why don't you take Aunt Claudia home. We can take care of things here." His gaze shifted back to Olivia. His first impression of her was right. Trouble was hot on her heels. He just hoped he could keep that trouble from taking over his town.

SEVEN

Olivia rolled over in bed and was instantly jarred awake by a sharp pain jabbing into her shoulder. She groaned and glanced at the small clock beside her. This was the third or fourth time she'd woken up since going to bed. At least this time she could take another pain pill.

She sat up and flicked on the bedside lamp. The guest room in the Morales house was comfortable and beautiful, with the same relaxed, rustic, Southwest feel as the main rooms downstairs. But it wasn't home. Who knew when she'd be able to get her furniture out of storage and settle down in one place again? She reached up to touch the area where she'd been shot. She shivered, even though the room wasn't cold.

The bottle of pain pills the hospital gave her sat on the dresser, but she'd need to go downstairs to the kitchen for a glass of water. Mentally thanking Claudia for packing an overnight bag for her, she reached for her robe at the foot of her bed. She tucked her good arm into a sleeve and let the fabric drape over her sore shoulder.

She headed toward the stairs, stepping softly on the thick carpet, trying not to wake anyone. But at the top of the stairs she could see dim light glowing down in the living room. Someone was already awake. Maybe they'd heard something. Dogs barking. A car engine prowling up the drive. The sound of someone ratcheting a shotgun.

Fear twisted her nerves from head to toe, turning the dull pain in her shoulder into a piercing jolt and setting her teeth on edge. She grabbed the banister with her good hand and started down the stairs.

Elijah sat on one of the leather sofas, his booted feet on the coffee table, watching the flatscreen TV on the wall with the volume turned down low. A laptop lay open with an electronic tablet beside it on the table in front of him. He had a pistol within reach on the sofa cushion.

Bobby sat at the dining room table, visible through the open, airy design of the common area. He was facing a laptop computer screen, the bluish glow reflecting on his glasses and giving his bright red hair a more muted, brownish appearance.

Jonathan, sprawled on the second living room couch, flipped the page of a thick paperback book.

Olivia reached the bottom of the stairs and all three of the men looked up. Elijah was on his feet in an instant. "What's wrong?"

"Something up?" Bobby asked, looking directly at her.

"I don't know." The sudden, intense attention was disorienting. "I was going to ask *you* if there was something wrong." Olivia looked for reassurance in the tense expression on Elijah's face. "Why are all of you awake?"

"Why are *you* awake?" Elijah asked.

Jonathan set his book aside and stood up.

"Did you hear something?" Elijah demanded, sounding like a battlefield commander. "Did you see something?"

"I don't see anything," Bobby said, his attention back on his computer.

"See anything? What are you looking at?" Confused, Olivia turned to Bobby, and then back to Elijah. "Do you have security cameras set up around your house?"

"What woke you up?" Elijah barked.

"My shoulder," Olivia barked back. She dug the bottle of pain pills out of her bathrobe pocket, held it up and rattled it. "I came downstairs to get a glass of water."

Elijah's shoulders relaxed slightly. She realized he had his pistol in his hand.

He tucked the gun into the waistband at the small of his back.

She sighed. Nothing like annoying the people trying to help you.

She walked by Bobby on the way to the kitchen and paused to see what he was looking at on his computer.

The screen was split into twelve images. She recognized the wooden crossbar at the entrance to the long driveway, the front door and a couple of views of the veranda at the back of the house. The other images were views of the outside of the house, and some other buildings, maybe a barn and a stable.

She looked up and saw Elijah watching her. "Who *are* you?" She gestured at the computer screen. "Why do you have so much security at your house?"

"It never hurts to be careful." He started toward the kitchen. "I'll get your water."

Olivia maneuvered around Bobby's chair so she could block Elijah's path. "Wait."

He stopped, his dark eyes intensely focused on her. Her mouth suddenly felt dry, but she held her ground.

"You already know a lot about me," she said. "You know a couple of humiliating things I would keep secret if I could. You know I lied about Ted Kurtz and you know I never gave Aunt Claudia the time of day until I needed her."

Olivia's eyes began to burn. Speaking that second truth aloud made her chest hurt.

Don't cry. You will not cry. She cleared her throat. "There are lots of things going on right now that I don't understand." Tears started leaking out despite her best efforts to hold them back. She awkwardly wiped them away with her good hand. "I think you should tell me something about yourself. And tell me why you're doing this for me. You don't even know me."

"She's got a point," Jonathan muttered.

Elijah shot him a brotherly glare. Jonathan picked up his book and sat back down.

When Elijah turned back to Olivia he took the pill bottle from her hand, glanced at the label and handed it back to her. "Come on," he said gently. "Let's get your water."

The shades were pulled down over the kitchen windows. An individual bulb in the vent hood over the stove was the only light left burning.

He filled a glass of water and handed it to her. While she took her pill, he opened the freezer and took out a half-gallon container of ice cream. "Caramel cashew," he said. "Your bottle didn't say you couldn't have food with your meds. Do you want some?"

"I never turn down ice cream."

He smiled and it looked good on him. It didn't soften his features as much as give them context. He wasn't an angry man, Olivia decided. He was just a very serious man most of the time.

She smiled back at him, letting her gaze meet his and lingering there for a few seconds.

Elijah turned away first. He opened a cabinet door and took out two bowls. While he was busy, Olivia found herself worrying about how she looked. Having to work one-handed, she did the best she could to smooth her hair and tuck some of the more unruly strands back behind her ears.

Elijah dished up the ice cream and carried the bowls to the breakfast table. Then he pulled out a chair for Olivia.

"It looks delicious," she said after they sat down. "But it doesn't get you out of answering my questions."

He savored a bite of ice cream before he answered. "Most of what Vanquish the Darkness does involves visiting people in the hospital, getting them outside and back into nature if we can, and just letting them know they aren't forgotten." He jammed his spoon back into the bowl and stirred his ice cream for a few seconds. "Sometimes we help people in a financial jam. Sometimes we run across someone in danger. In that case, the first thing we do is call the cops. But we like to offer a little extra support when we can."

He brought a spoonful of ice cream to his lips and let it hover in front of them. "We've brought people here before to keep them safe. It's made some bad guys angry. So that's why we need the extra security." He popped the ice cream into his mouth.

That was a very serious commitment to an outreach program.

"What about my second question? Why are you going out of your way for me? There are other members in Vanquish, other people you could have asked to help me."

He hunched over his ice cream. "You remind me of someone."

"Who?"

"A woman I was assigned to protect while I was in Afghanistan. Mrs. Elaine Somerset." He smiled slightly and shook his head. "She was a piece of work. She arrived courtesy of a charity organization, determined to make sure girls in Afghanistan got a decent education."

"A worthy goal," Olivia said, watching him closely. The confident expression he normally wore had begun to turn to something different, something more uncertain.

"I was her bodyguard for three weeks, then I was reassigned. There was a gap of time, very short, barely twenty-four hours, between when I left and when her new bodyguard would arrive." He stopped talking for a minute. "I had a bad feeling about leaving her unguarded, but I followed orders." He paused again. "I should have stayed to protect her, but I didn't."

Olivia was sorry she'd pressed him on the issue.

"Mrs. Somerset knew not to leave the secure complex where she lived and had an office," he said quietly. "And yet she did leave. To meet a reporter she knew who'd just arrived in Kabul." He paused again. "Both she and the reporter survived the acid attack, but Mrs. Somerset was severely burned." He took a breath. "She was splashed in the face and blinded."

Olivia's stomach sank. "You can't think that was your fault."

He shrugged. "She was a civilian in a dangerous place. Someone should have looked after her." He looked Olivia straight in the eye. "Just like someone should look after you. You're in over your head right now. You know that, right?"

"I do."

He gestured at her to eat. She took a bite of ice cream. It was delicious.

"I'm going on that job interview tomorrow at eleven," she said after a couple more spoonfuls.

Just so he knew her acceptance of his help didn't give him the last word on everything.

"Okay."

"We'll have to go by Aunt Claudia's first so I can get properly dressed for it."

"Understood. In the meantime, you might want to get back upstairs and get some more sleep." Elijah glanced at his watch. "Bedford will be here in about five hours. He'll probably have some tough questions for you."

Elijah glanced at his computer screen just before eight the next morning and took a sip of coffee. On the screen, Deputy Bedford made the turn from the road and drove his patrol car beneath the arch onto the Morales driveway. Somebody else was with him. A couple of minutes later Elijah was opening the door for Deputy Bedford and Sheriff Ben Wolfsinger. "Good morning."

"Morning." Bedford took off his department-issue cowboy hat while giving Elijah a nod. Wolfsinger, dressed in jeans and a long-sleeved dress shirt, likewise took off his cowboy hat and extended his hand to Elijah for a handshake. The gray at his temples gave him a distinguished look.

Elijah ushered them toward the couches in the living room. "There's coffee if you want some."

Both men declined.

Claudia sat on a couch with Olivia. Jonathan had fetched Claudia from her house and brought her over. Everyone else was at work or otherwise going about their daily routine. Elijah made the introductions between Olivia and Wolfsinger.

"How are you doing?" Wolfsinger asked in that focused way he had that made people feel their concerns were his concerns.

"Other than being shot at, I'm doing okay," she responded.

"I'm sorry that happened to you. But we're looking for who did this and we're going to find him."

Last night had been quiet after Olivia went back upstairs. She'd been surprisingly easy to talk to, and Elijah had found himself wondering about her personal life. He'd thought back through every conversation he'd had with her, trying to remember if she'd ever mentioned a man in her life. He didn't think she had.

Now, with Bedford and Wolfsinger here, maybe he'd get a clearer idea of what Olivia was facing and what he needed to do to protect her. As soon as everyone was situated in the living room, he turned to Wolfsinger and said, "Tell me you're closing in on Kurtz."

The sheriff sighed and turned to Olivia. "Who else wants to kill you besides Ted Kurtz?"

Olivia leaned back, staring at Wolfsinger with the wide-eyed expression of a woman confronted by a madman.

Elijah set his coffee mug on the table with a loud clang.

Olivia hadn't eaten more than a couple bites of her breakfast. She looked as if she hadn't slept very well, either. And she had that job interview she still insisted on going to. She didn't need any extra grief right now.

"Nobody else wants to kill me," Olivia finally answered, her voice brittle.

Elijah looked at the sheriff. He'd better have a good reason for asking that question.

"Nobody else has ever threatened to kill you?" Wolfsinger watched her closely.

"No, no one else has ever threatened me," Olivia said.

"Never?" Wolfsinger pressed. "You never had run-ins with irate husbands or boyfriends at that safe house? Or maybe after giving testimony in court or talking to the police?"

"Nothing I took seriously. I've had a few tense moments, but it was just angry people lashing out. The moment passed. Things moved on." She crossed her arms over her chest. "Why are you asking me this?"

"Because Ted Kurtz is out of the country," Wolfsinger answered. "He left ten days ago."

Her jaw dropped. But Elijah wasn't completely surprised by the news. He'd gone online and done some research last night. Like Bedford said the night Olivia arrived in town, it was hard to imagine designer-suited mob attorney Ted Kurtz skulking through the foothills around Painted Rock wearing a ski mask.

Olivia shook her head, refusing to accept what Wolfsinger was telling her. "Maybe Kurtz is just trying to make it look like he's out of the country."

"He's in the UK," Wolfsinger said. "I got confirmation this morning."

"Do you think he hired someone to kill me?" she asked faintly.

Sitting across from her, Elijah could see the tears well up in her eyes. And he could see the beginning signs of panic. She started to gasp, and then her chest began to heave as she fought back sobs.

"That's one of the scenarios we're looking into," Wolfsinger said. "But I don't want to rule anything out. If you could get the names of the men who threatened you because of your work at the shelter, we'd like to look into them, too. I'm sorry, but I have to ask again, who else might be angry enough with you to want you dead? An old boyfriend, maybe? A bitter ex-husband?

Did you borrow money from somebody and you can't pay them back?"

Much as Elijah wanted to protect Olivia and stop the hard questioning, he couldn't. They were painful questions, but given the circumstances, they were necessary.

"There's no one in my personal life who wants to kill me." Her voice had a hollow sound to it, as though her inner strength was dissolving. "I have a friend, Vanessa, who worked with me at the shelter. Maybe she can help me come up with some names of men who threatened me because of my work there."

"That would help. And I'm sorry for what happened to you."

She nodded. "I just want this to end."

He asked her a few more questions, many of them the same ones Elijah had heard Bedford ask right after she'd been shot. The sheriff was obviously hoping Olivia might have remembered some helpful detail she'd forgotten before, but that wasn't the case.

They wrapped things up and Elijah walked them to the door. Wolfsinger walked out first. Bedford stepped out, turned and lingered just beyond the door. "If she tells you anything that might help, you call us immediately."

"You think it's likely we're looking at a hired killer?" Elijah asked.

"I do. Watch your back." Bedford put his cowboy hat back on and headed toward his patrol car.

Elijah closed the door and walked back into the living room. Olivia sat staring off into space, biting her bottom lip.

She turned to Elijah. Her face had reddened and she'd started wringing her hands. "I don't know what to do."

She had to work through the emotions that came with having someone trying to kill her. Elijah knew that from experience. He just hated watching her go through it. But she needed to be reminded that she was strong, and a fighter.

"Does it look like you have to figure out what to do on your own?" Elijah asked, forcing an edge of disdain in his voice as he looked pointedly from Olivia to Claudia.

"No," Olivia answered sullenly.

"So work on that list of losers from the safe house for the sheriff's department to check out. Are you still up for that job interview?"

She squared her shoulders. "Of course."

"Then we'd better head over to Aunt Claudia's so you can get ready."

EIGHT

"I don't have a family ranching business to fall back on like *some* people, so this job opportunity is very important to me." Olivia hurried out of Claudia's house wearing her favorite suit, a navy blue light wool skirt and matching jacket with a black velvet collar and an ivory shell underneath. The last time she'd worn the ensemble it fit perfectly. Now the skirt sagged at the waist and the jacket was so loose she was easily able to get her bandaged arm into the sleeve.

"I understand this interview is important to you." Elijah followed her out onto the front porch and closed the door behind him. He reached out to grab her hand. The one attached to the shoulder that *hadn't* been shot. "But you need to slow down. Let me walk out ahead and see what's out there."

At least Olivia was pretty sure that's what he said. His strong hand holding hers suddenly brought her mile-a-minute interview-related thoughts to a screeching halt. The sudden sense of protection, the feeling of being cared for by someone as capable and earnest as Elijah Morales sent a gentle eddy of peace through her body that made her sigh.

And then a wave of dizziness took control of the moment. She caught her heel on an uneven board and might have pitched over into the bright pink zinnias at the bottom of the steps if Elijah hadn't tightened his grip.

"Do you want to go back in?" He turned her around and made her face him, his brows drawn down with concern. "We could call Larry and tell him you want to wait a week or two for the interview. He'd understand."

"I'm fine. My heel just got caught on the edge of a board." That was true. It was also true she got a little woozy now and then. Either from getting shot or from the pain medicine. But she wasn't talking to Elijah about that. He'd drag her back inside. She glanced past him at his truck parked in front of the house. "I'm fine."

"Larry's been looking for someone to fill that position for a while, so it's not like there's any rush." He let go of her hand. "Hard to believe, but there isn't a long line of people eager to move to a backwater like Painted Rock. Not for a part-time job teaching arts and crafts at a senior residential facility."

"I want the job." If it were an unpaid volunteer position, she'd still want it. Ever since Claudia had mentioned the job, she'd thought about activities she wanted to do, conversations she wanted to have. Maybe she could take some online classes and eventually work her way into counseling seniors. "I miss helping people. I miss doing something useful."

"A few of us from Vanquish ride up there to visit the seniors pretty often. I know Larry. He'll hold out for the right person. We can reschedule your interview.

"No!" She had to keep this appointment, had to get her life moving again. Now that she was injured, there weren't a lot of chores she could do to help Raymond around Claudia's ranch. Doing nothing productive and thinking about herself all day would make her miserable. She'd found that out while hiding in her apartment in Las Vegas.

"What if there's more than one right person for the job? I have to get there before Larry hires someone else." If Elijah wouldn't drive her she'd walk up there. Or find out if they had taxis in Painted Rock. "This might be my only chance to get back into doing the kind of work I love."

"You're too hard on yourself."

She let go a harsh, cynical laugh. "You're noble and you're good. People practically think you walk on water around here. I hear what people say about you. I've seen how they look at you." Her gaze dropped down to her feet. "You wouldn't understand what it's like to intentionally do the wrong thing, knowing it was wrong, and then have to live with all the pain and trouble you've caused."

He laughed softly, but when she looked up his expression had taken on an unexpected edge. The lines of his jaw looked tense as he leaned toward her, bringing his face close to hers. "Do you really think you're the only person around here who's done something to be ashamed of?" His voice was so quiet it was nearly a whisper.

"I'm sure whatever you did was in the course of a good cause," she said, starting down the steps, frustrated and angry with herself and tired of rehashing the same old topic over and over again. "Driving your motorcycle over the speed limit on the way to a fund-raiser for orphans won't get you on anybody's permanent naughty list."

He caught up with her, stepped past her, and then stopped, redirecting her into a sheltered corner of the wide porch. Getting her out of the potential line of fire if anyone was watching.

"I realize you just met me," he said. "But do I really give the impression I'm that shallow?"

She looked at the scars on his face, and then looked in his eyes. How could she have ever thought them flat and expressionless? The depth of feeling visible in them, the bottomless understanding coupled with the world-weary edginess of a man who'd seen it all, made her regret her snippy comment. "I'm sorry," she mumbled, looking away.

"If you're carrying around a burden of regret, this might be a good time to lay it down."

She laughed, but the bitterness coursing through her nearly turned the laugh into a snarl. "It's not that easy." She'd been a churchgoer. She'd heard the sermons about forgiveness generously given. But when you didn't really believe you deserved it, it felt impossible to receive.

"You don't strike me as the kind of girl who only does what's easy."

She blew out a breath and felt some of the tension leave her neck and shoulders. "Well, I am a girl who needs a paycheck. So, can we just go? I don't want to be late."

"Sure." He stepped back, took her arm and scanned the area around Claudia's circular drive while guiding her to his truck. He opened the door and helped her in.

"Maybe we should take your motorcycle," she said. "That would make a memorable impression."

Elijah got in the truck and started up the engine. "I thought you didn't like motorcycles."

"Yeah, well, maybe I'm getting a little more open-minded."

"I'll take you for a ride once things have settled down," he said.

"Thanks for doing this," she said as they started the short ride to the seniors facility. "I know you have your own job to do. I'm sure they miss your help around the ranch while you're dealing with me."

"It's no trouble."

A few minutes later, they pulled through the gate at Golden Sands, a rambling single-story building nestled between two rolling hills on the northern edge of town. Pine trees dotted the property, surrounded by wildflowers and rustling grasses turned golden in the early-autumn sun. Cultivated shrubs hugged the walkways alongside the building.

The chief administrator, Larry Squire, wore his long graying hair tied back in a ponytail. His shirt was tie-dyed in vivid shades of purple and orange. Olivia wondered if he'd made it himself as she sat in his office amidst scattered books, wind chimes, various clunky art projects and a guitar propped on a stand.

He stepped around his desk as soon as Olivia entered his office, and they sat in chairs across from each other for the interview. They talked about her prior job and she told him everything about her situation with Kurtz. He, in turn, had read about her getting shot in the local paper.

"I also read up on your situation in Las Vegas," he said. "While we have professional standards of behavior we need to follow, I know from personal experience that counseling can put you in a situation where you feel very protective of your client. Still, your history is a serious matter and it's something the board needs to consider before we can offer you employment."

"I understand, but you and the board should know I've learned my lesson." Olivia smoothed her skirt and crossed her arms.

"I know your aunt very well," Larry said. "I told her I'd interview you as a favor to her, but you would get the job, or not, on your own merits."

Olivia took a deep breath and prepared to be disappointed.

"I called a few of your references. Everyone had good things to say about you so I have to admit I'm interested." He stood up. "Let's go for a walk."

"Once we get further into fall and the animals start coming down from the hills, I'll have a whole bunch of new images I'll want to paint." Arthur Bannon turned back from the window to look at Elijah. Arthur's face was long and narrow, his hair still remarkably thick, though it had turned white, and his chin wavered slightly all the time. He was considered an old man when Elijah was still a schoolboy. He'd lived through a lot and earned every one of his ninety-two years.

Elijah glanced at his friend in his motorized wheelchair, pointing out the window at the rolling hills outside. While walking the grounds and waiting for Olivia's interview to conclude, Elijah had noticed the door propped open at the end of a window-lined building. Inside, he'd found Arthur.

"The only way I could paint a wildlife picture would be if the picture was already drawn on the canvas and someone jotted in little numbers telling me where to put each color of paint," Elijah said.

"You could paint a good picture if you really wanted to."

Elijah shrugged. "I'd rather let somebody else be the artist. I can just enjoy their work."

Arthur grinned and raised his bushy white brows. "If you've got fifty bucks, I've got a nice painting of an eagle soaring at sunrise that you could take home and enjoy. It's in a good frame, too."

Elijah looked down at Arthur's attempt at pleading puppy eyes and laughed. "Sold. I'll add it to my collection."

Arthur held out a freckled hand and they shook to seal the deal before Elijah pulled out his wallet.

Two sets of footsteps echoed down the interior hallway on the other side of the door connecting the art room to the main building. Elijah turned his gaze in that direction.

Olivia's vibrant laughter skittered down the hall. The interview must have gone well.

Olivia's eyebrows lifted in surprise when she walked into the room and spotted Elijah. The smile on her face beamed happiness that practically lit her up like a Christmas tree. She was so beautiful Elijah couldn't help smiling back. She gave him a lingering look before turning her attention to Arthur.

Larry stood beside her. "How are you?" he asked Elijah.

Elijah gestured at Arthur. "I'm about fifty bucks lighter in the wallet. Again."

Arthur grinned.

"This is the arts and crafts room," Larry said to Olivia. "And Arthur is an accomplished oil painter."

"Nice to meet you." Olivia walked over to shake hands with him. "My name's Olivia. I'm afraid I don't know a thing about oil painting."

"You don't need to." Arthur pushed his heavy, black-framed glasses up the bridge of his nose and studied her face. "I teach the painting classes. Rachel teaches quilting. Oliver teaches some kind of computer picture stuff that I don't care too much about."

"We have several skilled craftspeople and artists in town we can call on for help," Larry said.

"They just have to hire us some kind of babysitter," Arthur interjected. "And Larry told me he'd only bring a serious candidate down here to meet me so I guess you've got the job."

Olivia glanced at Larry. He pursed his lips. "I need to run it by the board, but I *will* recommend you. We'd like to have someone start within a week, if possible."

Olivia smiled broadly. "Thank you."

Arthur propelled his chair closer to Olivia for a better look, and then turned to Elijah. "Is she your girlfriend?"

Mortified, Elijah looked at Olivia, hoping she would answer. Instead, she sharpened her smile ever so slightly and raised an eyebrow.

Why did she do that? Elijah was good at reading the signs on a battlefield or behind enemy lines. He was good with horses and cattle, and was decent at weather prediction. He was a pretty good tracker, too. But he couldn't read women to save his life.

What did she want him to say? More importantly, why did he even care?

He didn't care. Did he? He was helping someone out, that's all. Protecting a woman in peril. He would do it for anybody. That was why he'd been allowed to survive when others hadn't. He had a debt to pay and a job to do.

For a moment he felt as if the ground was shifting beneath him. He'd helped women before. He'd kept his distance emotionally. He hadn't thought twice about it.

So what was happening with Olivia? Nothing, nothing was happening. He wouldn't let it.

Even Larry looked at him as if he was waiting for his answer. "No, sir," Elijah said to Arthur. "She is *not* my girlfriend." He blew out a subtle sigh of relief, thankful that was over.

"Why not?"

Really, Arthur? *Really?* The old man had a sharp glint in his eye.

They'd had variations on this conversation before. Not that Elijah had come up to visit with any other woman Arthur had mistaken for a girlfriend. It was the lack of a romantic attachment in his life that Arthur always bugged him about.

Elijah had been back home maybe a year when Arthur had started up about it. Arthur had been happily married for sixty-two years. His kids and grandkids came to visit him in Painted Rock at regular intervals. One mellow spring day Arthur had asked Elijah if he wanted a family of his own and in the unguarded moment Elijah had answered, "Maybe someday."

That was a mistake. Arthur wouldn't forget about it, and Elijah couldn't make him understand he wasn't anywhere near that "someday."

Elijah glanced at Olivia, watching for her reaction as he said, "I'm here with Olivia because she's run into some trouble. Vanquish the Darkness is helping her until things settle down."

Olivia's smile faltered and her radiant countenance dimmed. Elijah really didn't want to figure out why. He just wanted the awkward emotional stuff to go away.

"Have you asked her out?" Arthur pressed.

"You know I don't date." Elijah said.

"I still don't understand why not." The old man just would not give it up.

Elijah stared wordlessly at his normally well-mannered friend.

Olivia finally came to Elijah's rescue. "I just moved here from Las Vegas. Right now I'm not looking for a romantic attachment, either."

Arthur looked at each of them and shook his head sadly. Then he turned to Elijah. "Are you a complete fool?" He glanced down at the money still in his hand, then back at Elijah. "Life's for living, not for waiting around. When you aren't too busy to live a little, you come get me and bring me into town. I'll pop in my choppers and we'll get us a steak." He hooked his thumb toward Olivia, who was standing in the threshold of the outside door, admiring the view. "Maybe we'll invite her along, too."

"Deal," Elijah said. Anything to put an end to this topic of conversation.

Larry said his goodbyes and headed back to his office. Arthur drove his wheelchair to a window and pulled a sketch pad and some pencils out of a side pocket. Elijah was about to ask Olivia if she was ready to go when he saw something through the window behind Arthur. Something on the lightly forested hill just past the facility campus.

"Get inside," he barked out to Olivia.

She stepped back in the room. "What is it?"

"Maybe nothing." He strode to the window for a better look, mentally kicking himself for wandering off into "relationship land" and letting his feelings cloud his thinking about Olivia. There was no question as to whether they should date or have a romantic future together. He couldn't afford to be distracted like that.

Light flashed on the hill. A few seconds later he saw it again.

"You watching that light out there?" Arthur asked. "Probably just somebody driving on that old loop road."

"Probably." Elijah still didn't like it.

"I don't know why anybody would be out there now," Arthur continued, organizing his sketching supplies. "Nothing to see. Just a short drive around some trees. You wait until dusk, then you might see some critters coming out."

"You don't miss much," Elijah said, squeezing his friend's shoulder.

"These are for close up." Arthur tapped his glasses. "My distance sight is still pretty good."

Elijah got out his phone and hit a speed dial button while he walked outside for a better view.

"I called Jonathan and my dad," he explained to Olivia when he came back inside. "It might not be anything to worry about, but I don't want to take any chances. They'll be here in a few minutes to check things out before we leave."

The color had drained from Olivia's face and fear filled her eyes. Witnessing her beaming happiness just a few minutes ago made the return of her sadness even more punishing. Elijah hoped her tormentor was up there on that hill so he could track down the creep and end this nightmare for her today.

Arthur turned his chair and looked at her. "Why exactly did you move here from Las Vegas?"

Olivia reached over to rub her injured shoulder. "I made a mob attorney very angry with me."

Arthur raised his bushy white eyebrows and whistled. Then he shook his head and smiled wistfully at Elijah. "Boy, can you pick 'em."

NINE

"We spotted fresh tire tracks in the dirt up there," Joe Morales said through the rolled-down window of his truck, "but we didn't see anybody. Whoever made those tracks was already gone."

Jonathan sat in the truck beside him, scanning the hillside with a pair of binoculars.

Olivia sat beside Elijah in his truck in the Golden Sands parking lot. She looked through the windshield at the hill behind the senior center where they'd seen the flash of light just twenty minutes ago. "Thanks for looking," she called over to the other truck. She wished she could think of the words to express the real depth of her gratitude. The Morales family had done so much for her.

"Let's head back to the ranch," Elijah said.

Joe nodded. "Your brother went into town this morning and bought some heavy-duty locks. Make sure you grab them before you head to Aunt Claudia's."

"I will."

Joe wheeled his pickup truck around and headed out of the parking lot. Elijah followed.

"I don't suppose this rig has bulletproof windows," Olivia muttered as they picked up speed.

She looked at the passing landscape. In spite of the fear nipping at her, she could still see the beauty in the towering pines and the vistas of red mesas haloed by bright blue sky in the distance. She'd been shot, but she'd lived to see another day. She could let that drag her down or lift her up. Which was it going to be?

"If I spend much more time with you, I might have to get the whole truck armored," Elijah said.

She turned to him, her gaze tracing the strong line of his jaw. There was no hint of a smile, but she could hear the attempt at humor in his voice.

Her shoulder ached a little and she reached over to rub it.

"I'll do my best to keep you alive," Elijah said quietly.

"I know. And I'll do my best to keep myself from getting killed."

This time there was a smile on his lips. Just a little one.

They drove for a few more miles until he made the turn onto the Morales Ranch property.

Joe drove his truck toward the stables. Elijah steered toward a work shed near the house. "I need to grab a few tools before we head over to Aunt Claudia's." He cut the engine and climbed out of his truck.

"Can I help?" Olivia asked, climbing out, too.

"No, thanks. I've got it."

A few minutes later he loaded various pieces of equipment into his truck. Olivia's gaze lingered on one sharp-toothed, particularly mean-looking hunk of metal and plastic. "A chain saw?"

"I need it to clear away some of the hedges and tree branches around Aunt Claudia's house. Get rid of any good hiding places."

"Are you sure she'll be okay with you chopping up her plants?"

He turned to her. "You can't really think she'd value her plants more than you."

"I guess not." Olivia shrugged. "I just don't want to assume too much. I don't want her to be sorry she invited me to stay with her."

Elijah shook his head. "You don't know your aunt at all." He picked up a couple more power tools and put them in the truck. Olivia couldn't help admiring the muscles in his arms and across his chest as he moved with such easy strength.

"It's none of my business," he added, "but why didn't you or your family ever visit her?"

You're right. It isn't your business. Defensiveness burned through her like a flare and the harsh words were right there on the tip of her tongue, but she couldn't bring herself to say them. Not after all he'd done for her.

"Your family seems close," she said, diverting the conversation to a safer topic.

"Oh, we have our moments like any other family. Believe me." He slammed the tailgate shut. "Some days this ranch doesn't seem nearly big enough."

Jonathan exited a barn and walked toward them, pushing a motorcycle with a cardboard box balanced on the seat. When he got closer he picked up the box and dropped it into the back of Elijah's truck with a loud thud. "The locks," he said by way of explanation. "And Dad told me to wrap it up for the day and head over to Aunt Claudia's with you."

"Okay," Elijah said. "Let's go." He and Olivia climbed back into his truck.

Jonathan cranked up his bike and started out toward the road. Elijah followed.

By the time they reached Claudia's house, Olivia had turned Elijah's question about visiting Claudia over in her mind so many times that she wanted to say something. Just spit out a response and be finished with it.

"My parents weren't close to their families," she finally said. "I never heard of any particular reason why. Mom's family lives in California. Dad's family is scattered across Arizona. Claudia is his aunt. My parents never invested much time in visiting anybody, and by the time I'd grown up it seemed too awkward to try and track down any of my relatives."

"That's a shame. You missed a lot not coming up here for a visit. Uncle Hugh and Aunt Claudia always had time for kids. They were a lot of fun."

Olivia took a deep breath. Might as well get it all out there. The more she was around the Morales family, the more stories of her own life experiences stuck in her throat. And the more she missed being part of a family. "My family life disintegrated after my dad left my mom for another woman when I was seventeen."

"I'm sorry." He turned to look at her. "That had to be tough."

Funny how it still hurt all these years later. Just mentioning it, she felt the exact same sensation she'd felt when her parents first broke the news to her. As if she was falling and there was nothing she could grab hold of to stop the fall.

"Mom found someone and got married again a year later. I was eighteen. An adult. So they both had new lives, and I was on my own."

"You moved out of your mom's house?"

"Not right away. But it felt like I was by myself. I didn't have any brothers or sisters. Both my parents had started new relationships, gotten married, moved on."

"Without you?"

"I can't blame them. It wasn't like I was a kid anymore." But she'd still needed them.

"I still rely on my parents," Elijah said. "I doubt I'll ever outgrow that. It must have been lonely, not having that family connection to turn to."

She looked at him. Hard to believe that depth of understanding was coming from a tough-looking biker like him. "It was very lonely. I was desperate for company and started dating a man who seemed wonderful at the beginning," she continued. "After a while, I started to see flashes of temper in him, but I rationalized them away. Told myself everybody has their faults." She took a deep breath. Even now she didn't like thinking about Daniel and how bad things had gotten.

"I'm sorry," Elijah said. His voice was soft, but she could see the muscles flex in his jaw.

She shrugged off his sympathy, wanting to finish the story. "He shoved me a few times. Hard. I knew something was wrong, but at the time I felt like any connection with another human being was better than feeling alone."

"But you broke up with him."

She sighed and nodded. "Eventually. I worked

hard to rebuild my life after that. To make things better." She glanced out the side window. "I should have come out here. But Aunt Claudia didn't even cross my mind at the time. Instead, I prayed more than I ever had in my life. Eventually I found a therapist and that helped, too."

"So that's how you chose your career path?"

"I wanted to help people who were stuck in the same place I had been. Plenty of people say 'Let me know if you need anything' to someone in an obvious bind. They sincerely mean it, but you know what you really need if you're in serious trouble? You need someone to say 'here's a safe place to stay' or 'I brought you some groceries.' Something practical like that."

She turned to him. "You need someone to say, 'here's my cell phone and I'll wait with you until the tow truck comes.'"

He was quiet for a moment. "That's what Vanquish the Darkness does," he said.

And there it was. That emotional step back.

Subtle, but it was there. She got the hint. His help wasn't anything personal.

So be it. If Elijah wanted to keep her safe until the cops found whoever was after her, and then disappear from her life, that was fine with her.

Raymond walked up to the truck as they pulled into Claudia's driveway.

"What's going on?" he asked as Elijah grabbed

the chain saw from the bed of the truck and set it on the ground.

"Just going to do a little trimming."

"I take care of that around here." Raymond frowned. "Tell me what you need and I'll get it done."

"It's not for looks. I want to make sure there's no place for anybody to hide. And it needs to be done before it gets dark."

"I can do things to help look out for the ladies, too, you know." Raymond crossed his arms over his chest.

"I'm sure you can," Elijah said. "What I need you to do right now is check all the outside lights. I've brought a few spare bulbs if we need them. And we're going to install some stronger locks on all the house's exterior doors."

Jonathan, who'd arrived just ahead of them, grabbed a box of bulbs from the back of the truck and handed it to Raymond.

Raymond looked at them with a slight frown still on his lips.

"What can I do to help?" Olivia asked.

"Go inside." Elijah gestured for Jonathan to go with her. Then he scanned the area around the front of the house while he grabbed a pair of leather work gloves from the truck and put them on. He picked up the chain saw. "Rest your arm and shoulder."

"He's a real charmer sometimes," Raymond groused as Elijah strode toward the thick hedges where Claudia's property met the road.

"Yeah." Olivia watched Elijah walking away. *Yet he does have his moments.*

But then her thoughts drifted to the reason for all this activity. The shooter was still out there. And she didn't even know who he was. She didn't want to think about who might want to kill her other than Ted Kurtz, but she had to consider all the possibilities. The familiar feeling of claustrophobic panic she'd had while hiding in Las Vegas began to worm its way into the back of her mind, speeding up her pulse and making her feel as if she wanted to jump out of her own skin. She needed to get moving. Get her mind off herself.

"Maybe this is a good time for me to help clean up one of the sheds," she said. She gestured toward a wooden shed close to the house. "Organizing things helps me calm down when I have the jitters."

Raymond looked at her shoulder. "I don't think that's a good idea."

"I still have one good arm. At the very least I can take a look inside and come up with a plan to put things in order. And you and Elijah are right here. I won't be out here alone." She understood she needed to be careful. But she couldn't live with being caged up, spending her days hidden indoors. She'd promised herself when she left Las Vegas that she'd never put herself through that again.

"Well, if you want to clean up that dusty old shed, I'm not going to stop you," Raymond said.

Elijah powered up the chain saw, gunning the motor until the high-pitched whine sent Claudia's cats running from the flower bed.

"Those cats have the right idea," Olivia hollered above the noise. "Let's get away from this racket. I'll change clothes, then if you'll help me find some gloves I'll get to work."

"The outside lights are taken care of," Raymond reported to Elijah as the afternoon sunlight began darkening into early evening. "I've walked by every light fixture equipped with a motion sensor and made certain they all work."

"I upgraded all the locks," Jonathan said. He handed a ring with several keys over to Claudia.

Elijah nodded. "Good." He'd feel better when everyone was safely inside the house for the night.

It was almost dinnertime. Everyone was milling around in Claudia's kitchen. The tossed salad and a basket of rolls were already on the table. The only thing left was for Denise's tamale pie to finish baking in the oven.

"I got a few things straightened out in that shed by the north end of the house," Olivia said as she washed her good hand in the kitchen sink and splashed a little water on the other hand to rinse off the dust.

Elijah caught her eye as she dried her hands on a dish towel. He didn't smile at her. They'd already had one short, sharp conversation about her cleaning out that shed. He thought it was a foolish thing for her to do.

"I barely remember what's in that shed," Claudia said.

Olivia turned to her. "Let me go back out after dinner and finish it up before you look. I need to get the gloves I left out there, anyway."

"I'll finish it and I'll get your gloves for you," Elijah said.

"If you think it's dangerous for me to be out there, come with me."

Elijah nodded. He'd slip out there and take care of things for her after dinner.

A kitchen timer went off. Denise grabbed a couple of pot holders, took the tamale pie out of the oven and set it on the counter.

"Hiring someone to help with the cooking around here was one of the best decisions I ever made." Claudia leaned toward the casserole dish on the counter and sniffed. "It smells delicious."

"Oh, and here are the vitamins to take with your supper." Denise handed her a bottle.

"Oh, yeah. I'd forgotten about those."

"We all need reminders sometimes." Denise gave Elijah a significant look behind Claudia's back.

Elijah wasn't sure what it meant. Was she telling him Claudia had memory problems? He'd never noticed that. He glanced at Claudia. The passage of time demanded its toll from everybody. He should probably keep a closer eye on her.

Their workday done, Denise and Raymond left through the back door and headed for the cottage and their own dinner.

Claudia, Olivia, Jonathan and Elijah shared a quiet meal. Nobody wanted to talk about Ted Kurtz or the shooting, and for the moment Elijah left the topic alone. After they finished eating, Olivia sighed and pulled her phone from her pocket. "I should probably make some phone calls I've been avoiding. It's just after seven o'clock. Everybody should be home from work by now." She stood up and pushed in her chair. "If you want to leave the dishes, I'll clean up when I'm done."

Elijah watched her walk toward the den. She was moving in a kind of wobbly way. She'd done too much today.

"Thanks for taking her to the job interview," Claudia said.

"My pleasure." And he meant it—despite the occasional grumpiness, he enjoyed being around her. Elijah thought of her laugh back at the retirement center. Her kindness as she spoke to Arthur. The strength she showed in sharing with him about her family and the abusive relationship she'd been in. She was a strong, resilient woman.

Just then Olivia laughed.

"Who's she talking to?" Elijah asked.

Claudia raised an eyebrow. "Jealous?"

Jonathan snickered. Elijah glared at him until he stopped.

"Just curious." Olivia hadn't talked much about her life in Las Vegas. Had she left someone special behind? A man, maybe?

"She told me she was going to call her parents tonight."

"Good." Elijah stood and started collecting the plates. Maybe somehow this whole experience could help repair her relationship with her parents. Bring them closer together.

"After she talks to them, she mentioned that she's going to call a friend she used to work with at the women's shelter. A lawyer who volunteered there. She might have some news or ideas about who could be stalking Olivia other than Kurtz."

Jonathan stood and started helping Elijah clear the table. "That girl's been through a lot," Claudia said. "I'm afraid she's in too much of a hurry to get back to living a normal life."

Elijah thought the same thing. A few minutes later Olivia walked into the kitchen. Jonathan was filling the sink with soap and water while Claudia poured cat and dog food into colorful bowls. Elijah figured it was as good a time as any to talk about security. Jonathan would be sleeping on the sofa by the front door tonight. Elijah would take the daybed in the small office off the kitchen, near the back door. Both men would be armed.

"Stay away from the windows," he warned both women. "When you turn on the lights in your rooms, keep them low so you don't cast an obvious shadow."

Claudia nodded soberly.

Olivia began to chew on her bottom lip. Her phone chimed and she looked at the screen. "It's a text from my friend, Vanessa. I left a voice mail for her earlier. She should be home in a few minutes and she'll call me."

"Don't tell her too much about where you are," Elijah warned.

"Vanessa's the least of my worries."

Jonathan turned to Claudia. "Why don't you put your feet up and watch a movie? Take your mind off things. I'll take care of the dishes."

"Fine by me." Claudia settled down in the den with all three dogs and one cat. Elijah walked through the house, closing the blinds and turning down the lights. He also took the opportunity to bring in his rifle from the truck.

Jonathan had finished the dishes and Olivia was on her phone in the kitchen when Elijah came back, so he walked through the house again, double-checking that all the doors were bolted and the windows were locked. When he returned to the kitchen, Olivia was off the phone.

"Vanessa's booking a flight to Flagstaff." Olivia offered him a tired smile. "She'll be here tomorrow."

Elijah felt a low-level internal alarm go off. "I hope you told her to keep quiet about your location."

Olivia scoffed. "She's not going to say anything to anybody." She shoved the kitchen's swinging door open and walked toward the dining area at the front of the house. At the same time a light flickered outside. Someone was in the driveway.

"Get down!" Elijah grabbed Olivia's arm and pulled her beneath the wooden dining table. Then he sprang up to flick off the lights and grab his pistol from the end table where he'd set it. "Jon!" Standing to the side of the window, Elijah moved a corner of the curtain to peek outside.

Jonathan ran in from the den, gun in his hand. "What is it?"

Olivia's phone rang. She drew in an audible, ragged breath. "Looks like Deputy Bedford is calling." Her voice was shaky. She put the phone to her ear. "Hello."

Elijah's heart pounded in his chest. "Get Aunt Claudia!" he ordered his brother.

"It's all right," Olivia called out, starting to crawl out from beneath the table. "Deputy Bedford is outside. The lights are from his patrol car."

A knock sounded at the door. Furious, Elijah strode over to yank it open. "Maybe you could call *before* you drive up next time."

"I can do that," Bedford said evenly. He stepped into the foyer and stopped, nodding at Jonathan. "You two are staying here? Not a bad idea."

Claudia walked in from the den. "Good evening, Deputy. Is something wrong?"

"Sorry to bother you. I'm at the end of my shift and on my way home. I stopped by because I have some information I'm authorized to share with you." He turned to Olivia.

Elijah stepped up behind her. Just as a reminder he was there for her and she wasn't alone in this.

"The Feds have found ties between Kurtz and at least two professional killers," Bedford said. "One is named Lucas Powers. He works for a mobster Kurtz has defended several times and he's currently under surveillance in Los Angeles. The other assassin is only known via electronic media intercepts. The Feds have assigned him the colorful code name of Sidewinder. Right now there are no known details about Sidewinder. He, or she, is a complete mystery."

Elijah set his hand on Olivia's shoulder. He could feel her trembling.

"Thank you for letting me know," Olivia said quietly.

"You're welcome." He gave a slight nod. "Good night." Bedford left and Jonathan locked the door behind him.

"Professional killer," Jonathan muttered as they all stepped back into the living room.

Olivia gasped, her face suddenly red and her eyes brimming with tears. Claudia wrapped an arm around her and pulled her to her side.

"It's all right. Elijah's a professional, too," Jonathan said.

Elijah looked at him.

"Professionally trained soldier," Jonathan quickly added.

Olivia turned to Elijah. Fear haunted her eyes and tears rolled down her cheeks. His determination to protect her became an absolute conviction. The sheriff's department was doing all they could to hunt down the shooter. Until they succeeded, Elijah would stay by her side.

TEN

Olivia found herself drawn toward wakefulness from the depths of dreamless sleep. Something tugged at her, prodding her senses and demanding her attention.

She had a fleeting, watery image of a dark forest. Tents and lanterns and the scent of a campfire. The *very* strong scent of a campfire.

Aware that she was awake, eyes not yet open, she rolled over in bed and stretched. Strangely, she still smelled the campfire. Her eyes flew open as the terrifying realization exploded like a star. *Fire!*

She sat up and looked around her bedroom. The small lamp by her bed was still on. The book she'd been reading had slipped to the floor. She was still dressed in jeans and a T-shirt. She looked to the window where a sinister orange light rippled and waved at her through the spaces between the slats in the blinds.

After Deputy Bedford left and she'd had

a minute to just sit, her injured shoulder had started to throb. Elijah was right; she'd overdone it, but there was no way she'd admit that to him.

She'd taken a painkiller and watched a little bit of a movie with Aunt Claudia until her eyelids had gotten heavy. Then she'd gone upstairs to read. She must have fallen asleep.

Now she quickly got off the bed and strode over to the window to yank open the blinds.

The shed she'd worked in earlier was burning, surrounded by wiggling orange flames. Gray smoke speckled with glowing embers swirled and billowed into the night sky.

A fire department water tanker rumbled by the side of the house, firefighters already jumping off and jogging ahead toward the fire. The sensor-activated lights outside the bigger buildings were on, but the smoke was so thick it was hard to see anything that wasn't burning.

A couple pickup trucks drove past the house and parked near a barn. The occupants hurried out and grabbed shovels and rakes from the truck beds. Volunteer firefighters rushing to help.

Olivia needed to get out there and help, too.

She grabbed a pair of shoes off the floor and raced down the hall to Claudia's room to make sure she was okay.

"Aunt Claudia!" Olivia pounded on the door. "Aunt Claudia!" No answer. Fear flared through her chest and she pounded a few more times before opening the door.

A lamp glowed on a nightstand, showing Claudia's three pampered rescue dogs huddled on the rumpled bed. Otherwise, the room was empty.

Olivia pulled the door shut and headed for the stairs.

Several lamps were on downstairs and faint traces of smoke hovered in the air. She jogged to the kitchen, following the sound of voices.

Jonathan and Claudia were in the kitchen, talking while staring through the glass door at the flames.

"What happened?" Olivia cried out.

"Fire broke out maybe fifteen minutes ago," Claudia said, her voice a strange monotone. "Raymond called it in. Elijah was still awake, heard the commotion and went outside. Jonathan came and got me."

Oh, no! Poor Aunt Claudia.

"Why didn't anyone wake me?" Olivia demanded. "Let me get my shoes on." They were still in her hands. She grabbed a chair and plopped down. "I can go out there and help."

"I don't think so," Jonathan said quietly.

Olivia's head snapped up. "Why not?"

"Elijah told me to keep an eye on you and Aunt Claudia. And he specifically told me to keep *you* inside. The fire could be a diversion to get you to go out into the darkness where someone could grab you."

"You think this could be because of me?" Olivia asked, her rush of adrenaline suddenly bottoming out. And then a terrible realization struck her. "I left the light on," she whispered in horror.

"It's just a building," Claudia spoke calmly, barely acknowledging the anguish in Olivia's confession. "It can be replaced. But I am going to go check on my horses. We might need to move them."

Tears formed in the corners of Olivia's eyes. "I'm so sorry."

Claudia turned to her. "You didn't do this— it isn't your fault. Pull yourself together, honey. There isn't time for that."

For a moment Olivia could only stare at her great-aunt. Claudia's emotional and spiritual strength in the midst of a potential catastrophe was stunning.

"Don't even think about running away," Claudia added, her gaze so piercing Olivia felt as if her aunt was looking right through her. "This ranch is as good a place as any to make your stand. And don't think for a moment that I'm some feeble old thing who can't take care of herself. You and I are sticking together, come what may. Agreed?"

Olivia's jaw dropped slightly. Then, realizing Claudia was waiting for a response, she nodded her head. "Yes, ma'am."

Elijah stepped up to the storm door, yanked it open and walked in. White ash had settled all over him, cut by rivulets of sweat. He pulled off a helmet one of the volunteers must have given him and rubbed his fingers over his short, sweat-soaked hair.

"How bad does it look?" Claudia asked.

"The fire's obviously close, but it won't jump to the house. We're making sure of that. Mom and Dad are moving your horses away from the smoke and over to our place until we're certain none of the embers will start another fire. Whatever you had in that shed is lost."

"I don't care about the shed."

"Mark and Linda are heading a crew to put out any spot fires that pop up around the corral or the stables," Elijah added.

Claudia blew out a puff of air. "I need to get out there and have a look around. See what I can do." She squared her shoulders, shoved open the back door and walked outside.

Olivia turned to Elijah. "It's my fault," she said. "I left the light on in the shed. It must have shorted out and caused the fire."

Jenna Night   143

"That's not what happened. The light was still burning when Raymond and I first went out there and tried to put out the flames. We could smell kerosene."

"I must have kicked over—"

"No." He put his hands on her shoulders and looked her in the eye. "Someone had latched the door from outside. Dragged a section of an old plow in front of it. I think the shooter thought you were in there."

"He saw me earlier?" The realization made her knees start to buckle, but Elijah held her up.

"After you went upstairs, I went out there to get the gloves you were worried about. Yeah, you'd left the light on. But I left it on, too, when I came back to the house. I figured I'd go back out a little later and finish cleaning up. Next thing I knew, I heard Raymond hollering."

Elijah's hands were still on Olivia's shoulders and she leaned into him a little. That solid, self-certain way he had seeped into her and brought her a tiny measure of peace.

She needed it because it was still her fault. And it looked as though the torment was never going to end.

Elijah woke up on the narrow bed in the office off Claudia's kitchen feeling as if he'd chewed on nails all night.

The taste and smell of smoke still lingered in his nose and mouth, like stale water and ashes. And he'd only gotten a couple hours of sleep. Fitful sleep, at that.

The fire was out. Everybody was okay. The grounds behind the house were pretty well cleaned up. But worry for Olivia had needled him all night long. Images of what could have happened would flash through his mind and wake him.

Eventually, he'd fallen asleep for a couple of hours. But now the sun was coming up and it was time to get moving. He needed a cup of coffee. He also needed a plan to get through all his responsibilities for the dawning day.

Before anything else, though, he sat on the edge of his bed, closed his eyes and bowed his head to pray. It was the only way he could keep going, the only way he could do what he had to do. He'd learned that lesson a long time ago.

The coffeepot in the kitchen still held some of the leftover coffee Claudia had brewed for the firefighters last night. He was tempted to pour some of that into a mug and microwave it. Bad coffee and stale food offered a strange comfort. Maybe they were a reminder of days past, telling him how much worse things could be. Or maybe they just got him in the mood to prepare for battle.

In the end, he dumped out the old coffee and started a fresh pot. Eventually the others would wander in, and they'd want some. He grabbed one of Claudia's homemade muffins left out on the counter. She and Denise had pulled out every baked good they could find from every cabinet and freezer in the house and the cottage to make sure everyone who'd showed up to help fight the fire got a snack before they left.

Predictably, the cherry-pecan muffin was stale. But it hit the spot. While he chewed and watched the coffeepot gurgle, he thought about last night, mentally reviewing everything that had happened. What could he have done differently? What *should* he have done differently?

He thought about Olivia. He thought about her a lot. It was getting harder and harder not to. And that was a problem.

Plenty of people talked to him about "moving on" from his experiences in the army, and from the guilt he felt over coming home whole when so many were badly injured or didn't survive at all. His dad, his mom, his pastor and Arthur, of course, told him that he shouldn't dwell on the past—not if it kept him from living his life. But moving on, living a "normal" life, would mean leaving his fallen comrades behind. Letting their memory fade. And he would not do that.

He shook his head. Even if he was willing to

open up enough to try for a relationship, who said Olivia wanted someone like him, anyway? His scars weren't only on the outside. Right now she was afraid. It was natural for her to feel drawn to a man who was willing to help her. He was not the kind of man to take advantage of a vulnerable woman.

And how well did he really know her, anyway?

He plucked one of the dirty coffee mugs out of the sink, washed it, poured himself some coffee and forced his thoughts away from Olivia and back to the events of last night.

The first he'd known of the fire was when he'd heard Raymond yelling and then pounding on the kitchen door. Elijah had been on Claudia's computer, ordering supplies for his ranch. He'd yanked open the kitchen door and seen flames from the direction of the shed.

Denise had stumbled out of the cottage, talking into her phone, having already dialed 911.

Jonathan had run outside and Elijah had barked at him to stay in the house and keep an eye on Claudia and Olivia. Then he'd gone out with Raymond to turn on some garden hoses and try to keep the flames from spreading.

The shooter must have seen Olivia out there earlier. Maybe he had heard Elijah go in for Olivia's gloves. He must have assumed Olivia had returned to the shed to work for a while so he had gone to get the kerosene, shutting and blocking the door without looking inside to see no one was there before setting the fire.

Elijah took another sip of coffee while a question formed in his mind. What had Raymond heard or seen that made him aware of the fire? What, exactly, had woken him up? He would need to ask him.

The floorboards squeaked and Elijah looked over to see Olivia pushing open the swinging door between the kitchen and the dining room. Just before the door swung shut, he caught a glimpse of Jonathan sprawled on the living room couch, mouth hanging open, looking like a goofball.

Olivia was still wearing the jeans and T-shirt she'd had on last night. She must have collapsed into bed fully clothed, just as Elijah had done. Her hair was tied back in a disheveled ponytail.

Elijah stepped away from her and leaned against the counter. "Coffee?"

She nodded.

He washed out a coffee mug from the sink and filled it for her. When he turned around, she was rotating the arm of her injured shoulder.

"Looks like you're getting your range of motion back."

She reached for the mug he offered her and

took a couple of sips. "Yeah. It feels a lot better. I go back to the doctor in a few days and he'll tell me if I need physical therapy."

"How'd you sleep?"

She shrugged. "I don't remember."

"That's usually a good sign."

She looked into his eyes. Then her gaze shifted. He could tell she was looking at the scars on his face.

"From an IED," he said. "Improvised explosive device."

"Does it bother you to talk about it?"

"Not especially." There were things he didn't want to talk about. When that was the case, he had no problem slamming the door shut on the topic.

"It had to hurt," she said.

"I lived through it. Not everybody did."

"I'm sorry to hear that." She paused and looked at him, as if maybe she expected him to have something else to say about the subject. He didn't. But it was nice to know she would be willing to listen. Sometimes he did need to talk and not everybody could take hearing what he had to say.

He watched her walk over and pick up one of the muffins on the counter. She ate a bite, and then turned to him. "These things are stale."

"Yeah, but it's a good kind of stale."

She smiled. "Yeah, it is."

They stood there sipping their coffee and finishing their stale muffins in companionable silence.

Olivia poured him some more coffee, refilled her own mug, and then sat down on a round stool in the corner of the kitchen. "This can't go on," she said quietly.

Immediately his senses sharpened. "What, exactly?"

She looked down. "I can't keep disrupting everybody's life."

He watched her reach up to run her fingers through her hair. She felt around at the unkempt ponytail, pulled off the band holding it together and retied it.

Then she looked directly at him, studying his face again. It was somewhere between unnerving and intriguing when she did that. "I know you have a life and work to do at your ranch. Things to do besides follow me around."

He was a little concerned at where this was going. Was she reconsidering leaving? He set his coffee mug on the counter and crossed his arms. "What are you saying?"

"I'm saying I've been pretty self-centered, letting you drop everything to take care of me." She sighed. "If you want to go back to your own ranch for the day, I'll go with you. You could help your dad without worrying about my safety. Vanessa's flying in later this morning. There's no reason she can't go from the airport to your house. We'll all come back here when you're finished working."

He could get back to his usual routine for a day. Not spend so much time around Olivia. Have some time to get his head back on straight.

"Good idea," he said.

ELEVEN

"Wow. This is different from your apartment in Vegas."

"You don't know the half of it," Olivia said as Vanessa glanced around the living room of the Morales ranch house.

"I've traveled to northern Arizona before," Vanessa added, "but I've never had the good fortune to visit a ranch with a gorgeous view like this. I've got a few vacation days I've been ordered to use before they expire and I do believe I'll use them here."

If Olivia wasn't mistaken, Vanessa's gaze was lingering on the cowboys visible working outside. Elijah was one of them.

"Sorry I couldn't meet you at the airport," Olivia said. "But it's a long drive from here and, well, someone's been trying to kill me." It felt ridiculous saying the words aloud.

Vanessa turned and strode over to Olivia for another hug, having already swept her up in an

embrace as soon as she'd walked through the
Morales door.

She was a tiny little thing, decked out in expensive designer jeans, a silver knit top and
pointy-toed shoes with four-inch heels. She wore
her platinum curls piled high on her head and
when she came in close to hug Olivia she nearly
jabbed her in the eye with a red lacquered chopstick hair ornament.

"I'm so sorry this is happening to you," Vanessa said after she let go of her. "And we're going
to find the idiot who's doing this and nail him.
I promise."

Tiny and outlandish looking, Vanessa had already earned herself a reputation as a pit bull in
the courtroom. She'd told Olivia that she witnessed her stepdad hitting her mom on multiple
occasions when she was a kid. She'd grown up
tough. And she wanted to help people stuck in
domestic abuse situations, which was how she
came to meet Olivia.

"Thank you for the very sweet driver you sent
to pick me up at the airport, by the way," Vanessa added.

Bobby had been assigned that job. Upon arrival back at the Morales ranch he had escorted
Vanessa into the house, sat in a living room
chair, immediately picked up an electronic tablet and immersed himself in cyberspace. Olivia

got the impression he found Vanessa to be kind of intense.

"Bobby's part of that group you told me about, Vanquish the Darkness, right?"

At the sound of his name, he glanced up at them.

Olivia nodded. "He is."

"A Christian motorcycle group," Vanessa mused. "I had no idea such a thing existed. But I ran down everything I could find on Vanquish and they seem legit."

"Vanessa!"

"Hey, you're my friend and you're in trouble. You can't blame me for doing what I do."

"Wish I could say the same about your law firm," Bobby said, looking up from his tablet. "I mean about the legit part. Your legal firm has represented some pretty sketchy people."

Vanessa turned to him, frowning, hands on her hips. "Are you checking up on me?"

"Yes."

She broke into a broad grin. "Cool."

"Seriously?" Olivia looked back and forth between the two of them. "Does no one take anyone on face value anymore?"

"So, about your firm?" Bobby prompted, ignoring Olivia's small outburst.

Julie had brought in a tray with glasses of iced tea a few minutes earlier. Vanessa picked up a glass and took a sip. "When my firm hired me, they made it clear they believed everyone is entitled to a robust defense and if I didn't agree I could leave. I happen to agree. I'm not a personal fan of all of our clients, but I don't have to be."

Bobby looked ready to follow up on that, so Olivia hurried to change the subject. "Well, I just want you to know I appreciate you coming to see me." She gestured toward one of the couches. "Let's sit down."

"I figured it might not be safe to talk on the phone, so I had to come," Vanessa said, taking a seat. "Anyone who thinks their phone is secure these days is kidding herself."

The front door opened and Elijah walked in, looking every inch the cowboy in jeans and cowboy boots. He glanced at Bobby. "Thanks for the text." Then he introduced himself to Vanessa. "I wanted to hear what you had to say."

Vanessa's eyes practically glowed when she looked at him.

He walked over and sat next to Olivia, and for some stupid reason that made her feel better. Not that she had any kind of claim on him. Or wanted one.

"I don't have very many specifics to offer," Vanessa said.

"What does that mean?" Olivia asked.

"It means your local sheriff's department has

been calling Kurtz's law firm asking about him, his friends and his associates. I'm not sure if you know this, but Kurtz is out of the country. Vegas PD sent a couple of detectives to his office for a chat with some of the senior partners, at the request of your local sheriff, and that didn't make anybody happy." She flashed a sharklike smile.

"I thought Kurtz always liked attention," Olivia muttered.

"Not this kind. The state of Nevada is investigating him, too. Again. They've been trying to pull his license to practice law for years, but given his influential friends, they need to build an overwhelming case against him. The man has dirt on a lot of people that he wouldn't be afraid to use to his advantage." Vanessa glanced out the window, then turned to face Olivia.

"My sources tell me the state wants to build a full-blown criminal case against him," she continued. "Brutally attacking his wife and apparently getting away with it seems to be the last straw for a lot of people. Several useful anonymous tips have come in. If the investigators talk to you, maybe you'll be able to help build their case. You might know a small detail that's more important than you realize."

"I lied on the witness stand," Olivia said flatly. "I have no credibility."

"This isn't for a trial. An easily confirmed fact you could give them might connect him to a bigger picture."

"If Kurtz loses his legal license, he loses some of his value to his mobster friends," Elijah said. "That could be why he's so intent on coming after you. Or hiring somebody to come after you. Maybe he blames you for this new investigation. He could be nervous. Maybe he thinks you're outsmarting him and finding another way to get him locked up. It would be an added blow to his ego and he might not be able to handle that."

Olivia nodded. A bruised ego was the reason for a lot of the violence she saw at the shelter. Someone fearing a loss of control might lash out, too.

"I think the state investigation is the best explanation for why Kurtz would suddenly act so brazenly," Vanessa said. "The timing of the attacks lines up with that. If he's trying to take care of the problem himself, that might explain why things have been so messy. As far as I know, Kurtz has never actually murdered anyone. Do you know for a fact if he's in the UK? I'm just going by what his people are saying. They could be lying."

Olivia glanced at Elijah. Bedford had told them to keep that information to themselves.

"Do you have any other suspects?" Elijah asked.

"I'm still trying to get hold of a couple of parole officers I know so I can put together a list. Whether we're looking for Kurtz or someone else as our attacker, this looks like revenge violence to me. I see a fair amount of it in my work at the law firm. Trying to drive you off the road. Shooting you—but only hitting you in the shoulder. And now setting a fire. Bold, but not very efficient. Not very…well, professional."

"I'm glad he's not efficient. This is my life we're talking about," Olivia said.

"I know." Vanessa smiled sadly. "You remember Dan Vickers?"

Olivia nodded. "He came to the safe house looking for his wife and I called the police."

"And he threatened you."

"That man was full of hot air."

"He got paroled about a month ago."

"Considering everything else going on in his train wreck of a life, I have a hard time believing he'd even remember me."

"We're not talking about normal people who are just angry," Vanessa said. "We're talking about men who have crossed an important line.

They've used violence before—all of the men whose wives or girlfriends you met at the shelter. Or maybe these attacks have nothing to do with that at all."

Olivia felt her hopes for a quick solution begin to crumble. "You're a real buzzkill."

"Nature of the beast, kiddo. You're talking to a lawyer."

Elijah knew there was no point trying to see anything in the darkness of the night from the veranda behind his house later that evening, but he did it, anyway. Whoever was after Olivia might be out there right now, on the Morales property, watching.

That was why he had Olivia sit across from him, tucked into a corner formed by a trellis woven with night-blooming jasmine. No one lurking on the property would be able to see her. But they would see him. They would know he was watching out for her.

Elijah, Olivia, Mark and Linda, Bobby, and Jonathan were gathered at the back of the Morales house, seated on cushioned patio chairs, watching the flames die down in a fire pit on the veranda. The oncoming autumn night had a sharp bite to it.

Elijah watched Olivia in the fading firelight. Her face was fascinating, and he couldn't help staring. He liked the open, guileless expression he usually saw when he looked into her eyes. What you saw was what you got with Olivia Dillon. She wore her feelings on her sleeve and shared her thoughts whether you wanted her to or not. Her decision to lie to put Kurtz in jail must have weighed heavily on her.

Olivia had been quiet and pensive after Vanessa gave her report. And who could blame her? But shortly after dinner her demeanor had changed. She'd started smiling again.

She suddenly looked up and caught him staring. He looked away. He was supposed to protect her, not be fascinated by her.

After listening to Vanessa, he'd had Mark call his wife and ask her to drop by the Morales ranch after work. Franklin, who owned the Buckskin Bistro Grille in town, had also been available. Elijah wanted at least a few people from Vanquish the Darkness to be up to speed and ready to help in case anything new happened.

Because something *would* happen.

The guy tormenting Olivia wasn't going to stop. Elijah knew the type only too well. He would be fueled by Olivia's fear. Energized by hurting her. Eventually, he would kill her unless someone stopped him.

With extra people in the house, Julie had been unable to resist cooking for everybody. She'd barbecued beef ribs and they'd eaten outside on the veranda. After dinner, Elijah had gathered his troops and gone over what they knew. Vanessa stayed long enough to repeat what she'd told Olivia earlier, and then she'd gone inside the house to check her work email. She'd been there ever since. Franklin had gone into the house with Joe and Julie, offering to help package the leftovers from dinner.

Now those who'd stayed outside relaxed by the fire pit. Or tried to.

"What would Vanquish the Darkness be doing if you weren't watching me?" Olivia asked. She directed her question to Linda, but her tone set off alarms inside Elijah.

Linda sat beside her husband. Mark was the best, most natural cowboy on the ranch and more like a member of the Morales family than an employee.

"We have enough members that we can still do our normal activities and keep an eye out for you," Linda answered. "Next week we're holding a fund-raiser carnival at the high school in town. Tomorrow's Saturday, so we've got a ride scheduled. We're heading over to Quartz Creek. A nice man who's been through some rough times is finally getting back on his feet." She looked at Elijah. "You remember Dean."

Elijah nodded.

"He's reopening a small hobby and craft business he had to shutter for a while," she explained to Olivia. "It's his grand reopening so we're going to show up to support him and hopefully help attract some new patrons."

"I'd like to go with you," Olivia said.

"Maybe another trip," Elijah immediately countered. He knew where this was going. She was getting claustrophobic with all the protection. Unfortunately for her, it was going to get worse. He was not letting her out of his sight. He glanced into the darkness again. He was tempted to put on his night-vision goggles, but it would probably freak her out.

"No, not another trip," Olivia said calmly. "I want to go on *this* trip. Tomorrow. I can ride with Linda. If you don't mind," she said to Linda.

"I don't mind."

"You can ride behind us," Olivia quickly said to Elijah before he could object. "You can watch for anyone following us when we leave town. But I doubt that will happen. Whoever's after me wants to catch me alone. But I won't be alone."

"No way." Elijah needed to put a stop to this. "You'd be too easy a target on a bike. And you haven't been on a motorcycle before other than when I brought you to Aunt Claudia's after you got shot. It's a long way for a first real ride."

She turned back to Linda. "Do you have another vehicle going along? Like a car or a truck?"

Elijah felt his jaw muscles tighten and he shifted in his chair. It wasn't just the fact that Olivia was ignoring his advice that bothered him. That happened all the time when you were protecting someone. And it was fine with him that she was directing her questions to Linda. Linda was one of the most levelheaded people he knew. What concerned him was that Olivia was pointedly pushing him away. Why?

"We'll have a van going, carrying some coolers with food and sodas plus some gifts for Dean and his children. Franklin's wife, Darlene, will be driving it, and I'm sure she'd love the company."

"Perfect. Count me in."

"And that's our cue to get on home and get to bed early so we can get up and ride in the morning." Mark held out a hand and pulled his wife to her feet. She gave him a quick kiss on the tip of his nose.

Elijah felt a hint of longing for a relationship like theirs and immediately quashed it. He should be satisfied with the life he had. He'd returned from multiple tours overseas physically sound. Thanks to prayer and therapy, he was doing well spiritually and emotionally, too. Most of the time. His family loved and supported him.

He had no right to ask for anything more. In fact, he still had a lot to do to earn the blessings he'd already been given.

After ruthlessly killing that selfish twinge of longing for a family of his own, he took one more glance into the darkness as everyone filed into the house.

They all wandered toward the kitchen, looking for Joe and Julie to say their good-byes. In the midst of the hubbub, Elijah pulled Jonathan aside and asked him to find Vanessa, have her pack up her tablet and drive her to Claudia's house. He wanted a few minutes to talk to Olivia alone.

Olivia insisted on spending the night at Claudia's house. She said she'd made her aunt a promise and she wanted to stay with her as much as possible. So, a short time later, they were heading down the road in his truck, the seat between them filled with plates of food his mom wanted him to bring to Claudia.

"Tell me what's up," he said.

She turned to face him. "You have things to do besides shadow me. Your family has a ranch to run. They need you. Without your help, your dad and Jonathan and Mark and the other guys have to work twice as hard."

"It's good for them."

She made a scoffing noise. "After listening to

Vanessa, I realized this could go on for a while. I need to get to know some of the other members in Vanquish the Darkness. Maybe some of them could help me out sometimes." She was quiet for a moment, and then added, "Great, now I sound like a real user."

"No. Not a user. You sound smart. And they want to help you."

"So I'm not going to have to fight you on this?" she asked as they pulled up to Claudia's house. "You're not going to try to keep me from going tomorrow?" She blew a strand of hair from the front of her face. "That's a relief."

"No, we don't have to fight about it. But anytime you leave Claudia's house or my house, I *will* be by your side."

"Why? Why does it have to be you?"

"Because I'm better at the job than anybody else around here."

Obnoxious of him to say it, maybe, but he believed it was true.

Her face shuttered. She looked away.

"It's a good reason," he added lamely. But maybe not the entire reason. There was a small stubborn part of him that wanted to be the one with her because she added zest to his life. He fought the attraction, but it kept coming back. Since he'd met Olivia, he'd been painfully aware of how monotonous his life had become. He'd thought he liked it that way and had assumed he could live that way forever. Now the clear path to his future was starting to get a little foggy. He hated fog.

Claudia was already in the kitchen chatting with Jonathan and Vanessa when they walked in. Claudia had spent the day with friends and reported that she'd had a wonderful time.

"How are you holding up?" she asked Olivia.

"I'm fine. And I've got some great news."

A grin spread across her face and she held up her phone. "I got a text from Larry just after dinner. I got the job!"

What? Elijah turned to stare at her. So *that* was what was behind all this? She didn't want Elijah to go to work with her every day? She thought she'd replace him with other members of Vanquish? That's why she wanted to go on the ride tomorrow and get to know them?

Well, it was a nice try and a well-executed plan.

But it wasn't going to work.

He was going to accompany her every day for as long as it took to eliminate the person who was a threat to her. After that, she could do whatever she wanted to. Maybe she would move back to Las Vegas. That would make his life a whole lot easier.

TWELVE

"It feels good to be doing something useful for someone," Olivia said to Denise while peeling open a garbage bag and using it to line a plastic trash can.

Denise raised her eyebrows. "Whatever floats your boat."

Olivia paused on the cracked asphalt parking lot in front of Tinker Time Crafts and Hobbies and looked around. Quartz Creek was a hardscrabble little town without much in it. That was probably why the store's grand reopening had attracted such a good crowd.

Stay aware of your surroundings. Elijah's warning came back to her. It was part of the deal she'd agreed to so she could come on this road trip with Vanquish.

Colorful flag pennants tied to signs and light posts fluttered in the steady breeze. The riders from Vanquish the Darkness had lined up their bikes with perfect precision in front of the tinted glass windows with the store's name painted in metallic gold letters. Hamburgers and hot dogs sizzled on a barbecue. Popcorn popped in a small booth. Cool water and cans of iced soda were being passed around. And the man who had been introduced to Olivia as the proud owner of the shop was walking around profusely thanking everyone for being there.

Olivia was tempted to let go of fear and see only the happiness of the occasion. But she couldn't afford to do that. Not yet. Maybe someday.

Denise tucked a chunk of dark hair behind one ear.

"I can't think of the last time I saw someone so happy to change garbage bags," Denise said. "But good for you."

After hearing Olivia talk about the outing, Denise had offered to bake some goodies and donate them. At the last minute, she'd decided she wanted to go along and ride in the van with Olivia. Vanessa had stayed at Claudia's house to participate in a couple of conference calls for work. She still had a few more vacation days to use, but in typical workaholic fashion she couldn't stand to be out of touch with the latest developments in her cases back at the office.

Elijah and Mark had ridden their motorcycles behind the van, making sure no stranger followed them from Painted Rock. Everyone in Vanquish knew about Olivia's situation, and they were all keeping an eye out for her. Especially Elijah, who never wandered far away and oftentimes was already looking at her when she looked at him. Each time her gaze met his, she felt her face turn warm.

The sound of a child's squealing laughter caught her attention, and she looked toward a play area set up in the strip of grass beside the craft store. Kids chased each other through an inflatable castle, took turns at lawn bowling or fished for plastic goldfish in a wading pool. Members of Vanquish, decked out in their jeans, leather vests and heavy biker boots, wandered around and helped.

Olivia's gaze snagged on Elijah standing in a shaded, out-of-the-way spot at the end of the building. He was praying with a man and woman. The three of them stood holding hands, heads bowed. The woman's shoulders shook, as if she might be crying. The man's shoulders rose and fell as though he sighed deeply.

Olivia turned away, feeling like an intruder in an intimate moment. It was a stark reminder she wasn't the only person in the world facing trouble and fear.

"It's really great that you came to visit your aunt," Denise said as they walked to the next trash can overflowing with popcorn bags and hot dog wrappers.

"I shouldn't have taken so long." Olivia picked up some cups and papers from the ground, tossed them into the bag and pulled the drawstring tight.

"Claudia is getting up there in years," Denise said. "She takes some vitamin supplements to help with her memory, but I'm not sure they're working."

"Her memory?" Olivia stopped and turned her full attention to Denise. "Something's wrong with her memory?"

Denise shrugged. "If you're around her very much, you'll notice."

"Has she been to a doctor?"

"She doesn't go to the doctor. And if I mention it to anyone, they act like I'm insulting her. Maybe I am overstepping my boundaries." Denise crossed her arms and looked at the ground. "Her medical situation isn't really my business. But all these changes in her routine have made things harder for her."

"I'm disrupting her whole life, aren't I," Olivia asked with a sinking feeling as they started to walk back to the front of the store.

"I know you don't mean to," Denise said. "Your visit has brought her joy, too."

They reached the section of the parking lot

where Vanquish motorcycles were lined up in a row, chrome winking in the bright sunlight. Linda stood nearby.

"I should probably get back to the bake-sale table." Denise nodded a greeting at Linda and left.

A girl maybe nine years old walked up and stared at Linda's motorcycle. Along with lots of shiny chrome and an edgy, customized design, the bike also had a fascinating paint job. Among the airbrushed tree branches and leafy designs, were the hidden faces of Mark and Linda's four house cats.

"Do you see the cats?" Linda asked.

The girl nodded excitedly.

"This one's Loretta." Linda pointed to a tortoiseshell. "And this fluffy white one is Bubba."

"They're cute," the girl said shyly.

"Do you want to sit on the bike?" Linda glanced up. "If it's okay with your parents."

A man and woman had walked up behind the girl. The woman nodded. "Sure."

"I want to get on it, too." A rambunctious boy shoved past his parents and sister to get a better look at the bike.

"Hey, little man, I've got a ride you might want to have a look at." The voice belonged to Elijah, who'd walked over and stood grinning at the little guy.

The boy jumped up and down, landing on his mom's foot. "Cool!"

Elijah gestured toward his gleaming black chopper at the very end of the row of bikes. "I'd kinda like to see that one, myself," the dad said.

His wife kissed him on the cheek. "Go."

After the guys left, Linda held on to her motorcycle while the mom helped her daughter climb on.

"I want one of these," the girl declared almost immediately.

Her mother smiled broadly. "We'll see."

Olivia glanced over at Elijah. It looked as if he had his hands full with the rambunctious boy climbing all over him and his motorcycle, but Elijah was a natural—roughhousing with the boy just enough to help him burn some energy and give his exhausted-looking parents a break.

He would make a good dad. Olivia's heart ached sweetly at the thought. Underneath that lone-wolf biker image he liked to project was a man who loved family. She'd seen it for herself at the Morales household. And yet he was so determined to keep his distance.

It made no sense, but who was she to tell him how to live his life? Maybe he was just waiting for the right woman. One who wasn't a liar. He probably thought she was even more deceitful after the way she sprang the news that Larry had texted her a job offer. Maybe she shouldn't have surprised him that way, but she'd really wanted Claudia to know about it first.

In front of her, the little girl was ready to get off the motorcycle and Linda helped her down. Her dad was there a minute or two later, with the little boy and Elijah right behind him.

"Everything okay?" the dad asked.

The mom nodded. "Might be time for a break." They all expressed their thanks and headed over to sit in the grass.

Mark walked up and slid an arm around Linda's shoulders. "Having fun?" He kissed the top of her head.

"I am."

Olivia took a deep breath. The more she thought about the way she'd surprised Elijah with Larry's job offer, the more it bugged her. "Want to get something to eat?" she asked him. "I need to talk to you."

"Sure."

They said their goodbyes to Mark and Linda, and then walked over to the grill for burgers and chips. Elijah grabbed two sodas from an ice chest and they wandered over to the grass to sit.

"What's up?" Elijah asked before taking a bite of his burger.

"First, I want to thank you for everything you've done for me," she said.

He continued to chew, but his dark eyes suddenly locked onto her. He swallowed and took a sip of soda. "Where's this going?"

He was an intense man. It was easy to forget once you saw how kind and loving he was. But her first impression of him, as a man of strength behind a calm, measured exterior, was spot-on.

"I'm sorry I surprised you with Larry's job offer. I wasn't trying to be sneaky about it."

"Maybe you should put the job on hold and stay around the house until we find the shooter."

She had a feeling he was going to say something like that. She needed to explain again why this job was so important to her. Why she couldn't take a chance on losing it. "I blew it big-time in Vegas," she said. "When I left, I was afraid I'd never be able to work in the helping professions again. But now I have a chance to get back in. I want a job doing something meaningful."

He looked pointedly at the untouched burger on her plate. "Aren't you eating?"

She took a bite and chewed it. "The job at Golden Sands might be my only shot at a second chance."

"What are the hours?"

"It's only Mondays and Wednesdays to start." The next part was going to be hard to say, but she had to make herself say it. "I know they

need your help at the ranch. And I think maybe
you and I are spending too much time together."
She looked away, suddenly feeling shy. He had
to know exactly what she meant. "We should
probably take a step back." She glanced at him,
anxious for his reaction.

He nodded and kept eating.

Really? That was it? She put her heart out
there a little and that was his response?

"I've made a point of getting to know people
in Vanquish today," she said crisply. She needed
to step back from him all right. Right now she
couldn't step back fast enough. "Either the cops
or Vanessa will figure out who's trying to kill
me, and they'll send him to jail. I just need someone to ride with me to and from work, and keep
an eye on things until they catch him. Anyone
in Vanquish can do that, so you're off the hook."

He'd finished his hamburger and he wiped his
hands on a paper napkin. "I see."

"I've already talked to Raymond. He's driving me Monday."

"Is he?" Elijah cocked an eyebrow.

"Yes."

"Does your shoulder still hurt?"

"Huh?"

"The one where you got shot. Does it hurt?"

"A little bit. Why?"

"I just thought you might have forgotten about

it. You don't seem to realize that right now the shooter's setting the rules. He could take another shot at you anytime, any place." He glanced around. "Even here."

She stuck her legs out in front of her on the grass and studied the toes of her shoes. "That's not very comforting."

"It's not meant to be." He chomped on a potato chip. "Nothing's changed. Whoever's after you wants you to let your guard down. He wants you to believe you can go back to normal. You can't."

Two days later, bright and early on Monday morning, Olivia walked downstairs in Claudia's house. When she pushed open the swinging door to the kitchen, she found Elijah waiting for her. Her jaw dropped and she stopped dead in her tracks. The expression on her face was priceless.

Elijah fought back a grin.

She looked nice in a longish tan skirt made out of something that looked like suede but wasn't. Black boots. A blouse made out of light denim and lace. There were a few retired cowboys and cowgirls up at Golden Sands. Olivia would fit right in with them.

She'd been humming something when she first pushed open the swinging door. Elijah thought it might be one of the praise songs from the church service she, Claudia and Vanessa had attended with his family yesterday. But the humming stopped the second she saw him. Her gaze darted around the kitchen.

"Raymond's mucking out the stables," Elijah said. "I'm your ride."

The long, thoughtful look she gave him was a warning she was going to protest.

"You're not the only veteran in Vanquish," she finally said.

He'd seen her chatting with Vanquish members at church. She must have made some new friends.

"There are other riders who could go with me," she continued. "People with military or law-enforcement experience. People who know how to defend themselves and me."

"Raymond's not one of them—he wouldn't know what to do if something serious happened."

She sighed loudly. "Okay, you're right. I guess I still feel a little shy about asking someone in Vanquish. But I'll get over that. Give me the name of someone who doesn't work in the morning and I'll call them right now."

Fat chance. *He* wanted to be the one to see her in the morning.

It made no sense. It didn't fit into his life plans. He'd learned to push away hunger and fatigue and thirst in battle. Ignored physical pain. Why couldn't he push away this craving, too?

"Why don't you want me to go with you?" he finally asked. "Am I not charming company?"

She stared at him for a while as if she was waiting for him to say something more. Once again, he had the feeling she could see through him.

Finally, he pulled his keys out of his pocket. "You're going to be late for your first day."

The ride to Golden Sands was short and quiet. Olivia was only working a three-hour shift, so Elijah walked the grounds, made a few calls, then took his tablet and sat outside her classroom and got to work. The best part of being a cowboy was the riding and the roping. But there were still spreadsheets to keep updated, invoices to review, budgets to balance.

At eleven Olivia stepped outside her classroom. Arthur rolled out in his motorized wheelchair behind her.

"Glad to see we made it through the morning and you didn't have to shoot anybody," Arthur said to Elijah.

"The day's not over yet."

Olivia took a quick look around, but she also laughed. Elijah could tell she'd had a good first day. They said their goodbyes to Arthur and walked to the truck. Elijah scanned the surroundings as he helped her climb in and then walked around to get in on the driver's side.

"You have quite the collection of admirers here at the Golden Sands," Olivia said as they pulled out of the parking lot and started toward the Morales ranch so Elijah could get back to work. "Arthur and his friends thought it was their job to fill me in on all the gossip about you."

"That had to be boring."

"Arthur says you won't let yourself have a personal life. He says your parents are worried you won't let yourself move on from all the tragedy you witnessed overseas."

Elijah sighed. "Everybody has an opinion."

He knew his parents worried about him. They'd asked their pastor to talk to him more than once. He appreciated their concern. But right now he was a little irritated to find out the whole town talked about him behind his back.

None of them had any idea what they were asking him to do. The meaning of his life came from living it for people who were no longer here. And he would not let any of those people be forgotten. Keeping their memory alive gave his days their purpose and focus.

"So, are they right? Do you not want to have a family of your own?"

Some days Elijah admired her straightforwardness. Other days, like today, he wished she'd shut it down. "Not every man is cut out to be a family man. That doesn't mean there's something wrong with him."

"True. I just wondered. I saw you with that little boy on Saturday. He seemed like a handful, but you were good with him."

From the corner of his eye he could see her pulling an elastic band out of her purse and tying her hair back. Then she crossed her arms in front of her chest. She was gearing up for something. Great. Maybe he should have let somebody else drive her to work.

"That boy just needed to burn off some energy," Elijah said. "And he wanted some attention."

"I guess you figured out how to deal with kids when Jonathan was little."

"Yeah." He dealt with kids all the time through Vanquish. It wasn't a big deal. "Jon was a mellow little guy, just like he is now. Our sister, Amelia, is the wild child. We knew she was going to be a challenge from the time she was two."

Elijah glanced in his mirrors at regular intervals as they rode, making sure they weren't being followed.

"Losing people in battle doesn't mean you don't get to live your life," Olivia said.

Oh. This was what she was gearing up for. The conversation they were *not* going to have.

"You don't know what you're talking about," he said tightly. She didn't immediately respond. Good. That was the end of that.

"You're right, I haven't experienced what you have," she finally said calmly. "And if you want to live a life of duty and sacrifice, and choose to forgo a family life, that's absolutely your call. But it's absurd to think you're somehow paying back a debt to the soldiers who were lost or to God for being kept alive."

She might think it was absurd, but that was exactly how he felt. Elijah sat up a little straighter. He had a line. She'd crossed it. This conversation was *over*. "You need to focus on getting your own life together before lecturing me on mine," he said.

"You've got such a loyal fan club around here that no one will tell you the truth, but I will," she continued, undaunted. "You're being stupid."

Stupid?

"Well, that won't be your problem for long. I'm going to find this guy who's trying to kill you and neutralize him," Elijah said evenly. "After that you won't have to put up with me anymore."

"Okay, but can you hurry it up?" Olivia pulled down the mirror in front of her and checked her makeup. "You might want to bury yourself under obligation, but I had fun today. And I've decided I have a full life ahead of me to live."

Good for her. He could only hope she'd live it in Las Vegas. Or really, anywhere but here. With her gone, he could get back to focusing on the life he had chosen for himself.

"I don't leave anybody behind," he finally said.

He felt her watching him for a full minute before she spoke. "No one's asking you to do that," she said softly.

That's exactly what they were asking him to do. They just didn't realize it.

"Thanks for the advice." He shouldn't have tried explaining it to her. How could she possibly understand?

"You seem pretty comfortable handing out blunt advice whether people ask for it or not," Olivia said. "I figured I'd return the favor."

Elijah pressed the accelerator a little harder. The sooner they got to the ranch, the sooner he could get out of his truck. He'd keep his vow to stay by her side, but that didn't mean he had to stay within the sound of her voice.

THIRTEEN

Friday morning, Olivia watched Elijah as he sent Jonathan ahead to make sure no one was hiding on the other side of Elijah's truck. Olivia's checkup had gone well and her wounded shoulder was healing nicely. The trio was just leaving the doctor's office and she didn't think stopping for a celebratory lunch was too much to ask.

"I just texted Vanessa, and she said she's already in town," Olivia said, continuing to plead the case she'd started building in the lobby of the doctor's office. "She borrowed Aunt Claudia's car a couple of hours ago to run some errands."

"Let me think about it a little longer." Elijah put on his sunglasses. He seemed to be looking everywhere at once, as usual, but Olivia had spent enough time around him to know it didn't mean he wasn't listening. "Let's go get your car at Ricky's garage first."

Ricky had called last night to say her car was ready. Shortly after talking to him, she'd gotten a second bit of encouraging news. Sheriff Wolfsinger had phoned to tell her the FBI was stepping in to help with her case.

"Maybe the FBI profiler will be able to wrap things up quickly," Olivia said as she climbed into the truck.

"I'll be interested to hear what kind of person they think we should be looking for," Jonathan added as he shut the backseat door.

Elijah cranked up the engine and started to back out. "I doubt they'll share that information with us."

Probably not. But profiling was such a fascinating topic, even Denise and Raymond had hung around past their usual quitting time to join the conversation after Olivia got off the phone with the sheriff. Olivia glanced at Elijah as he made the turn onto Stagecoach Road. The tension that had developed between them after her first day at work had mellowed to an even-tempered temporary companionship. She hadn't tried to tread any further across the line into his personal life. He gave her as much personal space as possible while still keeping an eye on her.

Things had been quiet. No shots fired, no fires set, no overt threats of any kind.

It didn't take long to get to Ricky's Repairs and Towing. The business operated out of a gas station built in the 1940s that had been lovingly restored, like a collectible car, and given the addition of a modern six-bay repair facility.

All three of them walked into the lobby. A young woman in greasy overalls ambled in from the shop and offered her help. When Olivia gave her name, the mechanic gave her a compassionate look and said, "Ricky wanted to be sure he got to talk to you when you came in. I'll go get him."

The wall behind the service counter was made of glass. The repair wells and hydraulic lifts were clearly visible. Olivia could also see through an open roll-up door to her car parked in the lot out back. Her hands began to tremble and she couldn't take a deep breath. The sight of her car was a reminder of the terrifying night she'd been driven off the road. It was also a reminder of how hopeless and angry she'd felt when she left Las Vegas. How far she'd withdrawn herself from God.

Though He, of course, had never gone anywhere. And after her time spent with Claudia and Elijah and the Morales family, she found herself back talking to Him on a regular basis. Somehow, without Olivia realizing it, Claudia and her friends in Painted Rock had done a repair job on *her*. Even while someone was trying to kill her. Who would have thought that was possible?

Ricky came bounding into the front office, wiping grease off his hands with a red work cloth. "Hey!" he called out to Olivia. "Good to see you again."

"Good to see you, too."

"I heard you got shot." His smile collapsed into an embarrassed grimace. "But I've got to say you look okay."

Olivia smiled at him. "Thanks."

She handed him her credit card to settle the bill. Ricky swiped it on his register. While waiting for it to process, he talked to her about getting reimbursed through her insurance. He showed her where he'd noted that the damage was an act of vandalism on her work order.

He escorted them through the garage and out the back door toward her car. Elijah, as usual, looked all around as they walked.

"You want me to drive the car out to Aunt Claudia's?" Ricky asked, with a glance at Elijah.

"I can drive it," Olivia said, though she wasn't sure she wanted to.

"Or I can," Jonathan offered.

"Hey, when are you going to bring in that old motorcycle you're fixing up and let me help you with it?" Ricky asked Elijah, grabbing hold of his arm to get his attention.

Elijah turned toward him but he never got to answer.

An explosion sent a razor-edged shower of broken glass through the air.

In the seconds following the last of the blasts, Olivia felt entombed in absolute silence.

Slowly, she began to hear sounds. The tinkling of glass falling and breaking. Several car alarms going off. The groan of someone in pain.

The random impressions in her mind began to form into thoughts and she realized what had happened. Something must have blown up.

Some kind of pressure pushed down on most of her body where Elijah had dragged her to the ground. Had one of the garage walls collapsed? Maybe she was pinned under it. She slowly raised her head.

"Are you all right?" The pressure she'd felt lifted as Elijah got to his feet. He crouched beside her and put his hand on her shoulder.

She raised her head a little more and felt something like sand or gravel slide along the skin on the back of her head and her neck. "I think I'm okay." Her voice sounded strained, probably from the effort it took to draw in a breath. She'd had the wind knocked out of her, but she was finally able to push herself up to a sitting position.

"Wait, there's some glass." She felt Elijah

brush the back of her head and her shoulders. "Close your eyes and look down until I get this."

"What happened?" she asked with her eyes closed.

"Elijah!" It was Jonathan calling out from a few feet away.

"We're all right," Elijah called back. "You?"

"I'm okay. But Ricky's hurt."

Ricky was hurt? Olivia's blood turned cold. She started to stand up. "Somebody has to help him."

"Wait," Elijah commanded, putting his hand on her shoulder. "You'll be no help to anyone with glass and grit in your eyes."

He brushed the top of her head a couple more times. She heard sirens.

"Okay," Elijah finally said. "I think you're in good shape."

She shook her head a little, and then brushed her fingertips over her face and forehead feeling for glass. When she didn't feel anything, she carefully opened her eyes.

The first thing she saw was Elijah squatting beside her, one hand holding her good arm, the other hand holding a pistol. Her injured shoulder felt as if it was on fire, hurting nearly as badly as it had when she was originally shot. She must have fallen on it.

Gritting her teeth, she put the least amount of

pressure on it that she could as she tried to stand up. Elijah helped her.

Two sheriff's department patrol cars raced up and slammed to a halt at the corner in front of Ricky's shop. All other traffic had vanished. The deputies were out of their cars in an instant. One carried a pistol, the other a rifle. She thought the second one might be Deputy Bedford.

Crouching, the deputies ran around the shop toward the area behind the garage where she now stood. Dazedly, she tried to get her stunned brain to process what was happening.

A huge hole had been blasted through the back window of her car. The safety glass was all that had kept it from completely disintegrating. Her side windows were shattered and holes had been blasted through the back half of the body of her car.

Ricky's tow truck was parked near it, and its front window had been blown out, too. Whatever had hit it had also blown off the side mirror and ripped through the door.

Where was Ricky? Fear, mixed with nausea, rose up from the pit of Olivia's stomach. What had happened to him? She wanted to know, but she didn't want to know. And where was Jonathan?

She heard more sirens. Deputy Bedford spotted Elijah and spoke into the radio microphone at his collar. Still moving cautiously, he and the other deputy headed toward them.

"Elijah, what happened?" Bedford called out as he drew closer.

"Shotgun."

That was the source of the explosions? A shotgun? It had sounded like something a lot bigger.

Elijah still gripped Olivia's arm. With his other hand he held his pistol, now pointed at the ground. He gestured with his chin toward where the side street running alongside Ricky's shop intersected with Stagecoach Road. "He shot from that direction. I only saw one shooter. I'm pretty sure it was a man, but I couldn't see his face."

He'd turned and looked in the middle of all those explosions? Olivia thought he'd been crouched down, as she was.

They walked toward the tow truck where Olivia finally saw Ricky. He was sprawled on the ground and he looked frighteningly pale. He wasn't groaning anymore. She hoped he was still breathing. *Please, Lord, let him be alive.* One of the heavy side mirrors from his tow truck lay on the ground. Jonathan was kneeling beside him.

Bedford radioed for one of the EMS units positioned over on Stagecoach Road to move on in.

"Did that mirror hit him in the head?" Bedford asked.

"That's my guess."

"You see the shooter, Jon?" Elijah asked.

"No."

An ambulance rolled cautiously toward them.

Elijah tucked his pistol in his waistband, squatted down beside Ricky and put his hand on the man's shoulder. "Hey, bud, help is here," he said quietly.

Olivia didn't think Ricky was conscious. It was heartbreaking to see a young man who was normally boisterous and energetic lying so unnaturally still.

"Dear Lord," Elijah began quietly, as a paramedic hustled toward them, "we pray for Your protection and healing for our brother Ricky."

Olivia crouched down beside Ricky and put her hand on his shoulder as well, joining in Elijah's prayer.

She heard Jonathan whisper, "Amen," just as the medic got down on his knees by Ricky's side and started to assess him. Everyone got out of the way so he could do his work.

Law enforcement had already converged on the corner where the shooter had been.

The back door of Ricky's shop flew open and his mechanics ran out.

"Is he okay?" one of the mechanics asked, tears in his eyes, trying to get to Ricky's side.

Jonathan held him back. "Let's give them a minute."

"What happened?" the mechanic asked. Jonathan led him away, talking quietly to him.

Deputy Bedford turned to Olivia. "I'm going with the obvious assumption that this guy was after you and not Ricky," he said grimly. "Kurtz is still out of the country." He shook his head and looked around. "We aren't dealing with a professional killer. I'm certain of that now. It explains why everything's been so messy and ineffective from the beginning. What it doesn't explain is the sudden escalation. Your attacker has never gone after you when you were in a crowd before. Why now?"

"News travels fast in Painted Rock," Elijah said. "It's no secret the Feds are coming to help. Maybe the shooter heard about that and panicked."

"Maybe so."

A commotion from the side street caught Olivia's attention. Sheriff's department personnel had the intersection blocked off and they were putting up crime-scene tape, but someone was shouting. A few seconds later Vanessa came into view. She shoved her way around a cop trying to keep her back and ran across the asphalt, making a beeline for Olivia.

"All you all right?" she demanded. "I heard the sirens, and then saw all the cop cars and I was afraid something had happened to you."

Pain from her sore shoulder ricocheted throughout Olivia's body and she grimaced, then tried to smile for her friend. "I'm okay."

"No, you're not." Vanessa studied her face. "You have cuts on your forehead."

"It's nothing."

Still holding on to her, Vanessa turned to Elijah, and then looked toward the working medics. Her eyes grew even wider. She let go of Olivia's hands. "Is that Jonathan? Is he okay?"

"Jon's all right. That's Ricky—the mechanic."

"Who are you?" Bedford asked.

"Olivia's attorney," Vanessa said. "I've been in contact with Sheriff Wolfsinger about the attempts on Olivia's life. I gave him some names to look into."

Bedford gave her a long look. Then he turned and pointed to one of the deputies she'd run past. "You go back over there and wait."

Vanessa glared at him for a moment and then did as she was told.

"I'm so sorry I ever came to Painted Rock," Olivia said to the deputy. "I didn't mean to put anyone in danger."

Bedford gave her a sympathetic look before turning to speak to a fellow deputy.

The trembling in Olivia's hands began to take over her body. She faced Elijah.

He said something to her. She saw his lips move, but she couldn't hear him. She kept hearing the shotgun blasts all over again inside her head. She brought her hands up to her ears, trying in vain to block the phantom shots.

The medics loaded the gurney holding Ricky into the waiting ambulance. The driver hit the lights and sirens, and pulled out.

Olivia's knees started to wobble. Overwhelmed by her sense of responsibility for Ricky's injuries, she dropped to the ground. *Oh, Lord, please help Ricky.* She folded her hands tightly together, tears escaping her eyes and running down the sides of her nose. *And right now it feels so selfish to ask, but please, I need Your help, too.*

The next thing she knew Elijah was crouched down beside her. He wrapped an arm around her and helped her to her feet. She was starting to sob, drawing in noisy gulps of air as sorrow and regret slammed into her so hard, they felt like punches that rattled her bones.

Elijah gently turned her until she was facing him, then wrapped his arms around her. It felt as if he was holding her up. Not just physically, but emotionally, too. All of this was her fault and she knew it. Ricky was seriously injured. Who knew who else was going to get hurt before all of this was over?

There was so much she wanted to go back and do differently in her life, but she couldn't. Protected in Elijah's strong embrace she gave herself over to all the anguish she could no longer keep at bay. She was falling to pieces. For the moment, she let Elijah hold her together.

FOURTEEN

Elijah found a medic and had him look at Olivia's shoulder. The medic reached over to move her arm and Olivia yelped. "That's not a good sign," he said.

"I told you." Elijah crossed his arms and stared down at possibly the most stubborn woman he'd ever met. "It takes a while for a gunshot wound to heal properly."

"You're the lady who was shot?" the medic asked, his eyes widening slightly.

Olivia nodded. "Yes. But it's been a few days. I'm okay, just a little sore."

From what Elijah could see the wound wasn't bleeding, but that didn't mean Olivia was okay. He could tell that she'd been pushed beyond what she could stand. Running out of tears, pulling away from his embrace and pasting a forced, quivering smile on her lips didn't convince him that she was fine.

"Here, let me check out a couple of things,"

the medic said as he led her to an ambulance staged on a corner of Ricky's property.

He held her good arm as he led her over. Elijah followed closely. He watched the medic take her vital signs. Her eyes were red rimmed and her nose was swollen. Her cheeks and forehead were smudged with dirt and a little blood from where she'd scraped her chin. Despite all that he couldn't remember ever seeing a more attractive woman. Attractive in the real sense. His heart was drawn to her. More than he wanted it to be. Despite what he'd told himself about getting his emotions under control, he still wanted to be with her every moment he could. It was getting harder to imagine his life without her in it.

He'd almost lost her. Right here. In a split second when he'd let his attention be diverted from looking out for her.

Angry with himself for letting this happen, he could almost see Mrs. Somerset again, burned with acid back in Afghanistan. He'd failed miserably in his duty to protect that kind, good-hearted lady. He couldn't possibly let himself fail with Olivia.

While the medic continued to chat with Olivia, Elijah pulled out his phone and did a quick lookup for a number. He turned and walked away to make a call.

After he disconnected, he walked back in

time to hear the medic telling Olivia her vitals were good.

"Dr. Beamer can see you again at four-thirty," Elijah said.

"But I was just there." She shook her head. "I don't need to go back. I'm fine. Just a little sore."

"You can walk okay?"

"Sure."

He took her arm and helped her off the back of the ambulance. She winced a little bit, even though he was holding her good arm. "Do you feel like walking over there?" He nodded to indicate the corner where he'd seen the shooter. Bedford was already over there, along with some other deputies. "Or you could wait inside the shop here with Jonathan."

She turned to him, her green-brown eyes nearly liquid with emotion. "I want to know everything that's going on. I don't want to hide from the truth. It's better for me if I know." She cleared her throat. "Even if it's bad."

"All right."

He held her close beside him as they walked across the street.

The red brick building at the corner had been a bank a century ago. Now it was a furniture store. Elijah could see uniformed officers inside. Besides the county sheriff, the state highway patrol had a presence and he recognized a couple deputies from the neighboring county.

Elijah spotted Bedford on the sidewalk and walked up to him. "You have anything?"

The deputy shook his head. "We've got patrol cars out searching all over town, but there aren't any hot leads yet. Nobody saw a car speeding away. Nobody caught a glimpse of anybody with a gun fleeing the scene."

"Does this store have video surveillance?"

"Yeah, but only a single camera. Sheriff Wolfsinger is looking at the recording."

"The shooter could have walked through the store to the parking lot in back," Elijah said. "If he stayed calm, no one would have noticed him with everything else going on."

"We're talking to everyone in the store about everybody they remember seeing—whether they looked suspicious or not."

One of the other deputies called out to Bedford and he went into the store.

All the waiting and hiding since Olivia was shot had been eating at Elijah. Protecting her had become personal. He couldn't deny it anymore. He was certain he could track the guy who was after her, whoever he was. It was getting hard to stay out of it and let law enforcement do the job.

"Let's go." He wrapped his arm around Olivia's shoulder.

Bedford stepped out of the store and called out to them. "Don't go far. We need to get your statements."

"Don't take too long," Elijah answered back.

The shooter was no longer patiently waiting for a chance to get Olivia alone.

Things had just gotten a whole lot more dangerous.

"I know you'd rather go back to Aunt Claudia's house right now, but this makes things easier." Elijah drove his truck down the last couple of yards to the front of his family's house. "At least for the next few hours until things settle down."

Olivia nodded, even though she was fairly sure he wasn't looking at her. She certainly wasn't looking at him. He'd started badgering her to go to the Morales ranch rather than back to Claudia's house from the moment they left the doctor's office.

As she expected, the doctor told her today's shooting incident hadn't done any serious damage to her preexisting wound. Olivia had suggested she get a customer loyalty punch card for future use. Maybe the fifth treatment for getting shot at could be free.

It was either laugh or cry. But right now she wasn't laughing or crying. She was angry. She clenched her fists on the seat beside her until they went numb, and then let go, hoping the release would drain away some of the rage building within her. It didn't. She wasn't angry with Elijah. She was just angry with…*everything*.

"I told you if it made things safer for Aunt Claudia I'd come back to your house," Olivia finally responded.

"It makes things safer for you, too."

"You don't know that." She pressed her lips together and turned to him. His calm certainty was getting on her nerves. "Nobody knows what's going to happen next." She heard the shakiness in her voice and it fueled her anger. She turned back to glare through the front windshield at the Morales house. Its windows glowed with light in the early evening darkness.

How long was this going to go on? She was sick of being afraid. Tired of seeing other people get hurt. Angry enough to fight back. But she didn't know how or where to strike.

"The shooter might have killed Ricky," she said. Ricky wasn't out of the woods. He'd rallied on the way to the hospital, only to suddenly lapse back into unconsciousness. Last she heard, he'd been rushed into surgery.

A cold, sinking feeling crept through her, clinging to her head and the pit of her stomach. A sweet, kind, innocent man had been gravely injured simply because he was standing close to her at the wrong time.

"Ricky has a wife he adores and two little girls." Elijah spoke sharply, as though he thought Olivia was suggesting the young mechanic might die on purpose. "He's not giving up without a fight."

"A fight he wouldn't have to face if I weren't here."

"But you are here. We *want* you here."

She scoffed. The words came out so quickly it had to be one of the routine lines he gave everybody he helped. She reminded herself that all he'd done for her was routine— the same care he'd give to anyone. It wasn't personal.

Up ahead, the porch light was on. After the shotgun blasts, the day had taken such a frantic, terrifying turn that she wasn't sure what time it was. Six or seven o'clock, maybe.

True to his word, Deputy Bedford had gotten their statements fairly quickly. Bobby, Mark and Linda had met them outside the sheriff's substation and were following along behind them now, just to make sure they made it to the house okay. Jonathan and Vanessa had gone straight to the Morales place after Jonathan gave his statement.

Someone was trying to kill Olivia, yet at the same time complete strangers had appeared in her life to look out for her. She'd had someone by her side from the moment she'd first reached the outskirts of Painted Rock. She couldn't make sense of the greater plan, but all the help that had come her way couldn't be sheer coincidence. That thought helped to soften the edge of her anger. A little.

They pulled up to the house and Jonathan stepped through the front door onto the porch. Elijah parked the truck. Bobby, Mark and Linda drove their motorcycles around to a pole barn near the kitchen area of the house where there was a side entrance.

"Let me get your door," Elijah said. "I don't want you to move your arm."

He came around and helped her out of the truck. "You feel okay?"

"I feel fine," she said, not wanting to complain that the scrapes on her hands and face had started to sting a little. And she had a headache. She was so tired she could barely lift her feet. She was starting to tremble again, too. Fear and a sense of dark hopelessness gnawed at her. This was never going to end. Not until the shooter got what he wanted.

Elijah held her good arm as they started up the steps to the porch. His quiet strength showed her own dissolving defenses for what they were. Insubstantial and mostly faked. A sob grabbed hold of the center of her chest, like a clenched fist. Fear and anger threatened to choke her, but she didn't know how to let go of them. Especially not with a tough guy who'd been through a lot worse right there to witness her behavior.

When they reached the top step, Elijah stopped and turned to face her, wrapping both of his arms around her and pulling her carefully to his chest. Her face pressed into the warm skin of his neck just below his chin.

"Take a breath," he said quietly.

She tried to, but it was more of a gasp. Fear and anger fought inside her, and the trembling sensation she'd felt earlier became more of a shake. Hot tears collected in the corners of her eyes and rolled down her face.

"Try again."

With the second breath she felt stronger. She knew she had to do something to get this horrible, knotted-up feeling outside of her. Otherwise the black despair she'd felt in Las Vegas would come back with a vengeance.

So she did something ridiculous. It had absolutely no logic to it. She just decided on impulse to do it. She moved away from Elijah, reached down, pulled off a shoe and threw it as hard as she could at a nearby shed. It hit with a satisfying thud.

She immediately felt better. So she took off her other shoe and did the same thing. Another hard throw. Another thud. And an absurd feeling of relief.

"Do you feel better?" Elijah asked after giving her a minute or two to soak up the feeling.

"I do." She took a deep breath and squared her shoulders. "I feel better."

"Good."

She looked up into his dark eyes. She'd gotten so much better at reading the emotion there. He wasn't overly expressive, and that had been unnerving at first. Now it was comforting. At the moment she could see compassion there. But there was something else, too. Determination.

"I'm going to find whoever's doing this," he said.

Olivia shook her head. "No. We need to let the cops do their job."

He looked away, toward the shed. "Are you going to want those shoes back?"

She looked down at her stocking feet. "Well, I paid eighty-five bucks for them and I've only had them a couple of months."

"Okay." He sighed. "I'll go get them later."

"Thanks."

He reached out and ran the back of his finger

along her cheek down to her chin. The surface of her skin warmed.

"Ahem." Jonathan stepped out from the shadows.

Olivia immediately backed away from Elijah. Elijah shot his brother an annoyed look.

"Sorry," Jonathan said, a nervous smile on his face. "I was already out here when you two walked up."

"It's all right," Olivia said. "It's been a rough day."

"Yeah, it has." Jonathan turned to his brother. "Mom's right. You really know how to find trouble."

"Remind her not to worry."

"She's edgy because she's been fielding calls from Ricky's grandma for the last couple of hours. That's why I came out here to talk to you. You said you wanted to know as soon as there was any news."

"What's happened?" Olivia felt her stomach twist. "How is he?"

"He made it through surgery."

Hope began to blossom deep inside Olivia where there'd been none just a short time ago. "So he'll be okay?"

Jonathan shrugged. "We've just got to wait and see."

FIFTEEN

"How did the shooter get away without anyone seeing him?" Joe Morales asked a short time later. "It was broad daylight. Literally in the middle of town."

"I've been thinking about that, Dad." Elijah set his coffee cup on the end table beside him.

His mom's reaction to every crisis was to make a big dinner. Several people from church and from Vanquish had stopped by to offer their prayers and support, but all of them had resisted Julie's efforts to feed them and had kept their visits short. Once things settled down, Olivia, Claudia, Vanessa and the Morales family finally had a chance to eat. Bedford had called in the middle of dinner to say he and Sheriff Wolfsinger were coming over. Now everybody was in the expansive Morales living room, waiting for the lawmen to show up.

"A person can disguise their appearance easily enough," Elijah said, stretching out his legs and putting his booted feet on his chair's matching ottoman. "But hiding a shotgun? And hiding it quickly?" He shook his head. "I saw the cops looking around in the bushes to see if he'd tossed it. They haven't found anything, as far as I know."

"And why a shotgun?" Joe added. "It's hardly discreet, especially in that setting. That's raising the ante pretty dramatically. Why?"

Joe sat on one of the living room's long leather couches with Julie close beside him, her feet tucked beneath her. Elijah's mom wasn't someone who liked to sit still. Not unless she was very tired. Or very worried.

"Calling in the FBI has probably put the shooter in a panic," Elijah said. "He's desperate to finish the job before they get here."

He glanced at Olivia, sitting on the other couch with Claudia and Vanessa beside her. Her eyes were downcast and she looked pale. The uplifting effects of her outburst on the porch had vanished. She was worried about Ricky. They all were.

"Bedford and Wolfsinger are turning in at the gate," Jonathan said, looking at the screen of his laptop.

A few minutes later Jonathan got up to open the door for them.

"Sorry to bother you. I know it's been a long

day." Sheriff Wolfsinger was first through the door, his movements sharp and impatient. Bedford followed him in, taking off his cowboy hat and nodding a greeting to the group.

"We have some follow-up questions for Elijah and Olivia," Wolfsinger said.

Olivia sat up a little straighter. "I want to do anything I can to help."

Jonathan gave up his chair to the sheriff so he could sit close to her. Bedford remained standing and pulled a small notepad and pen out of his pocket. His demeanor was even more rigid than usual. The set of his jaws was tense and his eyes were narrowed. Elijah could read the signs. The deputy was angry and frustrated over what was happening in his town and wanted to bring it to an end.

"Tell me again what happened in Las Vegas," Wolfsinger said.

"Vegas?" Olivia said, her voice sounding puzzled. "Don't you want to know about what happened today?"

Hearing the confused vulnerability in her voice was like a punch in the gut for Elijah. But hard as it was, he kept his mouth shut. If the sheriff's department was on the trail of something, Elijah wasn't going to get in their way.

"Is there *anything* you haven't mentioned?"

Wolfsinger asked. "A detail I might need to know to save your life?"

"Do you usually accuse the victim?" Vanessa snapped. She stood up from the couch and walked around to stand directly behind Olivia.

"When we aren't making headway in an investigation, it often pays to back up and reexamine things from the beginning," Wolfsinger said evenly. He turned his full attention back to Olivia. "Perhaps we should talk in private."

"Certainly not without her lawyer present." Vanessa crossed her arms over her chest. Elijah could see why they called her a pit bull back in Vegas. "Have you checked on any of the names I gave you?"

"Yes," Bedford answered. "One of the men is a month overdue in checking in with his parole officer. There's an arrest warrant out for him but he was last seen in Rhode Island and he's had some pretty substantial health problems. I can't imagine him hiking the hills around here. The rest of the names on your list are accounted for." He returned his attention to Olivia. "We checked with the Feds to see if either of the professional killers we were concerned about were under surveillance at the time of the shooting. Just in case it actually was one of them. They'll get back to us."

Elijah was listening, but at the same time his

mind was replaying what had happened. He'd heard the first blast, shoved Olivia to the ground and thrown himself on top of her, covering her head and tucking down his own head. But then he'd looked up. And seen…what?

A swinging gray coat. A glimpse of someone's back as they disappeared around the corner. At that point he'd started to check on Olivia and the others. But he'd already told Bedford about all that.

"What leads do you have?" Elijah asked, rejoining the conversation. "You must have found some eyewitnesses by now. Physical evidence. Something."

"We've got very little," Wolfsinger answered. "People were minding their own business before the shooting. When the shots started, they took cover. Nobody saw anything. The guy just vanished."

"What about video cameras?" Olivia asked. "Security systems from the stores nearby?"

Vanessa eyed Wolfsinger and Bedford, and put a hand on Olivia's shoulder. "I'm sure they're already looking at that."

"The store on the corner only had one functioning camera and the images it captured weren't helpful." Bedford turned to Olivia. "When we put together what's been happening with what you tell us is the complete truth, it doesn't make much sense."

"The attacks seem emotionally driven and definitely not the work of a professional," Wolfsinger interjected. "Since all the potential enemies you told us about have been tracked down and accounted for, we think there must be someone you intentionally, or unintentionally, didn't tell us about."

"You think criminals always make sense?" Vanessa snapped.

"Ma'am, if I assume the person I'm after is crazy and acting completely randomly, there's not a whole lot I can do," Wolfsinger responded without taking his eyes off Olivia. "I work under the assumption that there's some piece of information or some bit of physical evidence I need to find that will tie the whole thing together. And then I'll catch my man. Or woman."

Wolfsinger stood, pulled a card out of his shirt pocket and jotted something on the back. Then he handed it to Olivia. "This is my personal cell number. If you think of something you want to tell me, call me."

Elijah could see Vanessa's eyes narrow. Wolfsinger's implication that Olivia was hindering the investigation by keeping secrets didn't make Elijah happy, either. But he understood the sheriff was just trying to do his job.

"I'm sure I don't need to tell you to be careful, but I'll do it, anyway," Wolfsinger said to Olivia as he and Bedford walked to the door. Wolfsinger hit a button on his phone and had it up to his ear before Olivia could respond. He walked outside.

Bedford lingered for a moment, running his hand through his dark blond hair before putting his cowboy hat back on. "You guys okay?" he asked, glancing at both Olivia and Elijah.

"We're all right," Olivia answered. "It's Ricky and his family who need your prayers."

"They've already got them."

"I should probably send the word out to everybody in Vanquish that we're not doing the fund-raiser next week," Jonathan said after Elijah closed and bolted the door behind Bedford. "Just so we have enough people available if we need their help."

"No." Olivia shook her head. "I can't ask everyone to be on call indefinitely." She took a deep breath and exhaled. "Other than the two mornings a week when I go to work, I'm not going to ask anyone from Vanquish to follow me around. I'll just come with you wherever you guys need to go. We can't let this creep ruin your fund-raiser. A lot of people depend on your support."

"Let's give it a little time and then make

our decision." Elijah didn't want to speak his thoughts aloud, but their plans would depend on whether or not Ricky pulled through.

"Can we go back to Aunt Claudia's house now?" Olivia asked. She looked down at her torn, grimy jeans and blouse. "I want to shower and change and climb into bed and hide there for the next week.

"Sure," Elijah said. He knew the feeling.

Olivia's phone rang. "It's Larry," she said, looking down at the screen before she answered. She became very still after a short exchange of greetings. "I understand," she said a minute later. She disconnected and stood staring at the floor. "He said in consideration of everything that's happened, the board of directors doesn't want me working at Golden Sands anymore."

Everyone in the room was silent. Elijah tried to think of something to say to make her feel better, but the words wouldn't come.

She finally lifted her face to look at him. Her eyes were watery and her nose was red. "My chance at starting a new job, restarting a meaningful career is all gone." Her tone was flat and bitter. "Whoever is doing this has finally succeeded in taking everything away from me."

"This is a bad idea." Olivia gazed uneasily around the interior of the Painted Rock High

School gymnasium, site of the Vanquish the Darkness annual fall festival. Her eyes looked especially large in her pale, thin face. Ricky was on the road to recovery, but worry over him had taken its toll on her nevertheless. Meanwhile, worry over Olivia had convinced Elijah he needed to take her someplace with a light-hearted atmosphere.

"Look at all the people here." She faced Elijah. "What if the jerk who's after me takes another shot while I'm here?"

"All the members of Vanquish know to keep an eye out for trouble. They're watching the entrances, the parking lot and the field out back where the rest of the festival is set up."

Elijah hoped a description of all the precautions they'd taken would make her feel better. And the truth was, she wouldn't be any safer at Claudia's house or the Morales ranch than she was here. No amount of safeguards could stop someone truly determined to do harm. "Sheriff Wolfsinger sent a reserve deputy. He's parked outside on the south lawn. The kids can sit in his patrol car and hit the siren if they want to."

"How can anybody keep an eye out for the shooter when they don't even know who they're looking for?" Olivia asked.

"Sadly, that's something professionals have to do all the time these days."

They walked to the middle of the cavernous gym. Bright balloons and glittery streamers hung from the crossbeams just below the ceiling, gently swaying in the delicate shifting currents of the room. When Olivia stopped, Elijah took an extra half step to bring himself closer to her. Maybe in a few days, when she'd had time to recover, he'd tell her a little bit about his time overseas. Maybe tell her a story or two about a brother-in-arms who hadn't made it back. But he'd keep it light. Make it a funny story. So many of the things he remembered were sad, but when he tried, he could think of memories that made him laugh or smile, too. It might be time to share a couple of them, to remember those old friends in a happier light, for a change. See how things went.

"Hey, you were the one who insisted we not cancel this shindig." He nudged Olivia lightly with his elbow. "And you were right." He gestured toward a grinning boy sitting in a chair, having his face painted so he looked like a lion. "That little guy is having fun. Maybe you could have a little fun, too."

She looked at the boy, but her expression didn't change.

"I should have left town after Larry fired me." She frowned and looked over at two girls and a mom playing a ring-toss game. "I shouldn't have let you talk me into staying."

"I know Vanessa invited you to go back to Las Vegas with her when she left, but hiding out in her apartment is hardly a golden opportunity. You'd only do the same thing you're doing here. Stay inside or under guard until the shooter is caught."

She was on the verge of leaving town. Elijah could sense it. And if she wanted to go, there wasn't a thing he could do to stop her. Well, he *could* stop her, but it might get him thrown in jail.

The sheriff's department hadn't given out any public information since the downtown shooting other than to confirm that the FBI profiler would be arriving in town within a couple of days.

Elijah glanced over at Olivia. Maybe the festival was too much, too soon.

"If you want to get out of here, I can take you back to our ranch or Aunt Claudia's house."

"No, thanks. I'm all right." She glanced toward Linda and Jonathan by the side and back doors, and Mark at the front entrance. "You go ahead and mingle. There are plenty of people keeping an eye on me." She lifted her chin and forced a thin smile.

"Pshew! I made it!" Claudia marched up carrying a couple of shopping bags overflowing with stuff she'd made out of colored yarn. Elijah's parents followed behind her, toting more overflowing bags.

"It's good to see you out of the house, honey." Claudia bent down and gave Olivia a peck on the cheek. She turned to Elijah. "Where do I set up?" She set down a bag and dug a card out of her skirt pocket. "I'm at table twenty-four. Is that in here or outside?"

One of the festival organizers suddenly appeared at her side, smiling. "I can help you."

Startled, Olivia jolted away from the man and stared at him, her eyes wide with fear.

"What?" Elijah looked at the man. Jason Ruger was a Painted Rock native who'd lived in town for all his sixty-three years. He was no threat. "Is there something about Jason that looks familiar?" Elijah demanded. "Something about his appearance that reminds you of the shooter?"

She didn't answer. Jason turned to Elijah and smiled nervously.

"Talk to me," Elijah snapped. Who else was in her line of sight? He scanned the room, senses on full alert. Maybe she wasn't staring at Jason. Maybe it was someone behind him who'd awakened some unconscious memory.

He rested his hand on the handle of the pistol

tucked into the waistband of his jeans beneath his shirt. "Tell me what you're looking at."

Olivia finally tore her gaze away from Jason. She blinked several times, and then looked around at the people now staring at her. "I'm sorry," she said dazedly to Elijah, and then to Jason. "I don't know what happened. I just panicked for a minute." Her face was flushed. She looked down.

"What scared you?" Elijah asked, moving his hand away from his gun.

"It's hot in here." She brushed her forehead with the back of her wrist. "It's nothing, really— I just didn't realize he was there until he started talking. For a minute, it was like I was back on that sidewalk in Vegas with Ted Kurtz suddenly beside me, threatening me. It felt like it was happening all over again."

"Understandable," Elijah said. "You've been under a lot of stress for a pretty good while."

"I'm so sorry," she said to Jason. "I feel like an idiot."

Jason tilted his head slightly. "No need to apologize. If I'd been through the things you've suffered through, I'd be a nervous wreck, too. The whole town will breathe easier when that criminal gets caught." He turned to Claudia, glancing at her shopping bags. "You didn't bake this time?"

"Denise baked some cookies and scones," Claudia said. "She and Raymond are here somewhere."

"Glad to hear it. I hope that means they're interested in joining us at Sunday services."

"Maybe." Claudia shrugged. "They told me that considering all that's been happening, they wanted to help." Claudia glanced at the card in her hand. "Table twenty-four?"

"That's outside. Follow me."

Elijah watched them go. His mom and dad trailed behind, still toting Claudia's bags.

"I can't do this anymore," Olivia said quietly.

Again, Elijah found himself searching for words he didn't have. Words that would make her stay. He never counseled women in his work with Vanquish the Darkness. Rescue them? Yes. Protect them? Definitely. Do anything that required muscle or a cool head? Absolutely. But, counsel women? Listen to their deepest feelings and respond with whatever words they needed to hear? No. Never. He'd fend off the bad guys and then hand the women off to other, more empathetic members of Vanquish the Darkness to help with all the emotional stuff.

But he couldn't do that with Olivia. He couldn't let her go, send her to someone else for the reassurance she needed. Much as it challenged him, he wanted to be the one who heard how she felt. And he wanted to be the one to make it better.

He'd done a lot of thinking over the past few days. That foggy road to his future had started to clear up and some of the things people had been saying to him for the past couple of years were finally sinking in to his hard head. Maybe it was time to tear down that wall he'd built around himself after he got out of the army.

God wasn't looking for him to sacrifice living a full life as penance for having survived. His fallen buddies would tell him he was an idiot if he walked away from a woman like Olivia. Maybe the answer to his fear of leaving them behind was to share his memories with more people. Maybe even his own kids, one day. Then there would be even more people to help keep those stories of valor and sacrifice alive. Keep those memories alive.

Guilt had held him back for too long. It was no different from the guilt he saw Olivia holding on to. Guilt she needed to let go of before it dragged her down.

"You *will* get through this," he said. "I'll help you. Just hold on for a little while longer."

She crossed her arms over her chest, as though she was literally trying to hold herself together.

"Come on," Elijah said, putting an arm around her shoulder. "I'll take you home."

"No." She looked steadier, but she was still very pale. "I made it this far, I'm not backing out now."

The pride and admiration in his heart made him want to lean down and press his lips against hers, but the middle of the fall fund-raiser didn't seem like the right time or place. He settled for reaching over and brushing his finger along the soft curve of her cheek. She reached up and rested her hand atop his. "Let's just find a place to sit down and get something cool to drink."

"Good idea." Elijah breathed a sigh of relief. She still might bolt back to Las Vegas, but at least it didn't look as if she was leaving tonight.

SIXTEEN

"That went well." Elijah pulled his truck out of the high school parking lot behind his brother and in front of his parents and Claudia. Raymond and Denise had stayed behind to help clean up.

"It was fun," Olivia agreed. Elijah turned to look at her with his eyebrows raised and she laughed. Okay, so maybe she'd had a moment of misplaced drama with poor Mr. Ruger, but she had gotten over it. "It was kind of overwhelming to find myself in the middle of a crowd again, but I had a good time. And you've got to admit I got pretty good at that ring-toss game."

"The one designed for three-year-olds?"

"Yeah, well, I've never had the best hand-eye coordination in the world. It was a little challenging at first."

"You're not serious."

She didn't answer.

"You *are* serious?"

She tilted her head back against the headrest and laughed, enjoying the soothing warmth of the moment. "I really was kinda proud of myself each time I got a ring around the neck of one of those bowling pins."

She turned to look at Elijah. His eyes were on the road and he wore a slight smile.

She'd wanted to sit in a corner and hide after humiliating herself with her irrational reaction to Jason. Elijah had let her quietly hide for a few minutes but not for long. And then he'd encouraged her to help out. Soon she was meeting people he'd known his whole life, laughing and relaxing and having a good time. She'd eaten too much junk food and gotten pink cotton candy stuck to her shirt and time had flown by. Before she knew it, the fair was winding down.

"At least the weather held out for us," Elijah said as a sudden gust of wind buffeted the truck and sent a couple of spidery-looking tumbleweeds bouncing across the highway in front of them. Dark clouds twisted in the sky overhead and large drops of rain began to splatter on the windshield.

Up ahead, Jonathan's brake lights flared as he slowed and made the turn into Claudia's driveway. Halfway down the driveway, he suddenly stopped.

Elijah steered to the right to pull up alongside

him. As he did, his lights shone across the front of the house.

"What's that?" Olivia asked, sitting up straight. The truck lights reflected oddly on the front windows, glowing in strange angles.

"I don't know," Elijah answered in a low voice. The wind from the approaching storm, increasing in fury, blew the curtains back and forth. Jonathan moved his truck, pointing his headlights toward the front door. It gaped open halfway off its hinges. The bulb in the motion-sensor light by the front door was visibly broken.

A few seconds later, Elijah's parents pulled into the circular drive behind them. From their vehicle's movements, first normal and fluid, then slow and tentative, Olivia could guess the moment when they realized something was wrong.

"Oh, my," Olivia said slowly. She couldn't have uttered an additional word if she'd wanted to. It felt as if the wind whipping around had somehow managed to steal her breath. What must it look like inside the house? What had happened? Her stomach turned to lead. This wasn't just storm damage. It was something much more sinister.

She reached for the handle and pushed the truck door open. Suddenly she felt Elijah's arm like an iron rail flung across her body.

"Wait." He pulled her door closed. His phone

rang. He answered it, turning in the direction of his parents. "I see it," he said without preamble. He listened for a few seconds, and then glanced at Olivia. "I'll bring her over to you. If you and Mom can get Olivia and Aunt Claudia out of here, Jonathan and I will go in and have a look around." He disconnected.

Olivia stared at him as she slowly realized why he didn't want her to get out of the truck. Shock and fear turned her body numb. "You're going in?"

He nodded.

Jonathan was already looking in their direction. Elijah pointed at his brother, then himself, then the house. Jonathan nodded his understanding.

Thunder boomed overhead and harder rain began pelting the car, bouncing off the metal with a sharp pinging sound.

"Shouldn't we call the sheriff?" Olivia asked, terrified to think who or what might be inside the house. A bomb. An IED. Some deranged person with a shotgun pointed at the door.

"You call it in as soon as I get you in Dad's truck," Elijah said. "Let's go."

"No!" Fear rose up in her as she looked at the dark house through the rain, and then back at him. "Just wait for the sheriff."

"I can't."

"Why not?" she practically wailed. "It might be a trap."

He looked at her with dark, hardened eyes. "You're right. It might be a trap and we've already tripped it. There might be somebody in there who will start shooting if we just sit here. Or if we try to drive away."

"No," she said miserably. "No. This can't be happening."

"Sometimes doing nothing isn't the safest thing," Elijah said. "This is one of those times."

Joe Morales pulled up his truck behind them. "Come on," Elijah said, and before she could register what was happening, he'd come around the truck and pulled her out into the rain. Holding her arm tight and close, shielding her body with his, he hurried her to his father's truck where she could see Claudia, ashen faced, sitting in the backseat.

Elijah pulled open the door and helped Olivia inside. "I'll have Jonathan hang back on the porch while I go in," Elijah said to his dad through the open driver's door window. Rain was starting to run down his face, but he didn't seem to notice. "When you see me go in the door, drive off as fast as you can. If there's anybody in there, I'll distract them."

"Be careful, son."

Elijah nodded once, then turned and headed

for the house, taking out his gun. Jonathan got out of his truck and followed him.

Julie had already called 911.

Everything seemed to flash by in seconds yet take hours to unfold. Olivia watched Elijah go to the front door, crouch down, then go inside. *Please protect him Lord. Please.*

Julie was talking to a 911 operator when Joe hit the gas and tore out of the driveway.

Thunder rumbled and lightning flashed overhead, tossing shadows around Claudia's vandalized living room and illuminating blades of broken glass scattered across the floor. Looking for trip wires, Elijah moved slowly and avoided stepping on anything other than exposed wooden floor.

Someone had gone through the house in a fury, tearing up everything in their path. The sofa and easy chairs had been sliced, their stuffing thrown everywhere. Lamps were overturned and broken, potted plants toppled over, pictures ripped down from the walls, thrown to the floor and stomped on until the glass cracked.

The front room curtains, made heavy by the rainwater, continued to whip back and forth through the broken front window. They'd already swept the nearby shelves clear, knocking the little ceramic dogs and cats Claudia collected to the floor.

Elijah continued through the dining area. The dining-table chairs were torn, their stuffing ripped out. He hesitated by the swinging door to the kitchen. He drew in a centering breath. The weight of the gun in his hand reassured him.

Something moved on the other side of the door in the kitchen. Elijah heard a soft, rhythmic sound. Like someone walking.

The surface of his skin tingled and his heartbeat sped up with a familiar thrum of excitement. A smile of anticipation formed on his lips. The hunt was on. *Finally.*

He shoved the door open and crouched down low. A flash of lightning gave a glimpse of cabinet doors hanging open, broken plates and glasses on the floor, cereal and flour and dried pasta and some kind of shiny, syrupy substance thrown everywhere.

He pressed his back against the wall beside the swinging door, trying to peer into the darkness. His senses focused, he tried to read the room, listening for breathing, trying to feel the presence of another human being, anticipating where his quarry might be hiding. Muscles tensed, he pressed away from the wall to peer around an open cabinet door.

He heard the sound again, only this time he

recognized it. It was only the rhythmic tapping of the screen door being blown back and forth by the gusting wind. For the next few seconds the loud boom of thunder swallowed the sound.

If Elijah were setting a trap, this is where he'd do it. He'd wait for his prey to see the door left open in the storm, then let down his guard to walk over and close it. That would be the point when he'd take his shot.

So he stayed crouched low, using the open cabinet doors for cover as much as possible, inching forward while trying not to rattle any of the pots and pans strewn across the floor. He reached the entrance to the small office that served as his temporary bedroom and crept inside, listening for the sounds of breathing. Trying to catch a glimpse of the smallest movement. A few books on the shelves had been flung to the floor, but nothing worse had been done here. It was a tiny room. It didn't take long to confirm it was empty.

What a disappointment.

Now convinced there was no one hiding in the shadows waiting there to kill him, he went to the back door and looked out. The motion-sensor lights in the back of the house had been broken. The falling rain was turning into a torrent. He stepped out on the concrete stoop and looked around but couldn't see signs of anyone.

Any footprints that might have been left behind had already washed away.

He stepped back into the kitchen and closed the door behind him. The light fixture on the ceiling was still intact so he flipped a switch. The light came on.

"Elijah?" It was Jonathan's voice.

Elijah walked back to the living room and crossed the foyer. He held up a staying hand to his brother, who was still on the front porch. "Wait here." He continued through to check out the rest of the first floor, still cautious but not overly optimistic that he'd find anyone. There were things pulled off the shelves in other rooms, but compared to the front of the house, the effort looked halfhearted. Maybe they'd been in a hurry to finish up and get out.

He went back to the foyer and waved Jonathan in. Wide-eyed astonishment and outrage flashed across his brother's face. Emotions Elijah couldn't afford to let himself feel right now.

"Stay here," he said quietly to Jonathan. "And don't touch anything," he snapped as his brother righted an overturned end table. "Let the cops see it first." He glanced toward the staircase. "I'm going upstairs to have a look."

"Maybe we should wait for the cops."

"I'm just going to make sure nobody's up there. Be right back."

He headed up the stairs. The first few family pictures on the wall alongside the staircase had been knocked down and Elijah stepped around them. At the same time he kept an eye out for anything that might be rigged as an explosive. In the stairwell, away from the bright lightning flashes, his eyes grew accustomed to the dim light. Inching his way up, he tested each step before putting his full weight on it.

All three bedroom doors upstairs were closed. The first room to the left was Claudia's. He turned the handle, shoved the door open and backed away. A small warm light glowed faintly, and the next thing he knew he heard a series of thumps and the pattering of feet. Lots of feet. All three of Claudia's dogs scampered up to him, whining joyfully and wiggling in greeting.

"Hi, guys," he said quietly. He glanced around the room, and then stepped inside. A night-light glowed softly from a wall socket. The center of Claudia's bed, rumpled, showed signs of recently holding a trio of spoiled dogs. The closet door was ajar. He pushed it open and saw both of the cats curled in a clothes hamper. They were awake, but apparently too comfortable to move. The room looked otherwise untouched.

"You're better off in here," Elijah said, giving each dog a pat before slowly exiting the room and softly shutting the door behind him.

Olivia's room and Claudia's crafts room were likewise undisturbed. And empty.

His phone chirped as he headed back down the stairs. A text from Bedford. He was waiting outside. Elijah and Jonathan needed to get outside *now* before one of the deputies accidentally shot them.

"Come on," he said to his brother when he got to the door. Outside, four sheriff's department patrol cars were parked in Claudia's driveway, in stealth mode, with the engines idling but all their lights turned off. Elijah walked out into the pelting rain and waved them in.

Bedford and his fellow deputies made quick work of checking out the house, taking pictures and dusting for prints. Elijah was allowed inside while they worked, but Bedford sent Jonathan home.

"You might want to move everybody back to your place for a few days," Bedford said after Elijah finished answering his questions. "This isn't just about tearing up a house." He glanced around the living room. "This is a message. He's telling you he can come in here and get Olivia anytime he wants to."

Elijah had gotten that message.

"It looks like a lot of effort went into breaking the family pictures on the walls and shelves," Bedford added. "Maybe that means something.

Or maybe it was just a quick and easy way to make a mess."

"Is it all right if everybody comes back now?" Elijah asked.

Bedford nodded.

Elijah took out his phone and sent his parents and Jonathan a quick text.

"Do you have any updates on Ted Kurtz?" Elijah asked as he slid his phone back into his pocket.

"He's still in the UK. I'll get an alert when he leaves."

"Any chance you did a background check on Olivia's friend Vanessa?"

Bedford nodded.

"Well?"

The deputy hesitated slightly before answering. "Did you know Vanessa worked at the same law firm as Kurtz a few years ago?"

"No." But hearing that fact did stir up a memory. Hadn't Vanessa said something about Kurtz having a hold over people? That he could blackmail them into doing favors for him?

Claudia stepped through the front door a few minutes later with Julie beside her.

The deputies had left the light above the stairs on and someone had propped open the swinging door from the kitchen so light shone out from there, as well. The women looked at the damage inside the house while Elijah looked at the sad, stunned expressions on their faces.

Claudia slowly looked upward toward her bedroom.

"The dogs are fine," Elijah quickly reassured her. The expression on her face shifted. He expected tears. Instead, he saw her brows lower and her chin jut out slightly. He knew that expression from the days when she was irritated with her husband. Claudia was itching for a fight.

"Where's Olivia?" Elijah asked.

"Right behind us." Julie sounded puzzled, as if she couldn't accept what she was seeing as she glanced around the interior of the house.

He moved past his mom out to the darkened porch where Olivia stood staring at a broken window. Jonathan was beside her. When he saw Elijah, he raised his eyebrows slightly. Elijah gave a quick nod, and his brother turned and hurried back down the steps toward the parked trucks.

"You okay?" Elijah asked. He wanted to reach out and take her in his arms, promise her he would find whoever did this. He wanted to kiss away the worried expression on her face. But maybe she didn't want him to. Maybe after this she'd finally lost faith in him and his ability to protect her.

"Sometimes it takes a while to track down whoever you're after," he said. "But it doesn't mean you give up. Or that you run away. You know that, right?"

She nodded, but she still wasn't looking at him.

Behind her, in Claudia's driveway, he saw Bobby's SUV. Mark and Linda were there, as well. Jonathan was helping Joe grab some tools and lumber from the back of his truck.

"Dad and Jonathan will have these windows boarded up in no time," Elijah said. He needed to keep everybody's morale high. Whoever did this wanted to make everyone feel defeated. Elijah was not going to let that happen.

Olivia still didn't respond. This wasn't a good time for her to dive back into that pool of self-pity or regret or whatever dark emotion was beckoning her. They had things to do.

He crossed his arms over his chest. "So why exactly are we standing out here with the rain blowing on us?"

She took a deep breath and let her shoulders drop. "He was here. In Aunt Claudia's house. In the place that's my *home* now." She lifted her hand, reaching forward past the point where the window used to be. "He's not going away. He'll be back."

Elijah couldn't let her give up hope. And he

didn't want her to even toy with the idea of leaving. He'd gotten used to seeing her every day. Missed her when she wasn't around. Whether she was smiling at him or telling him what for, she'd managed to open a heart that he'd thought was permanently closed off a long time ago.

As soon as he found who'd been tormenting her and he neutralized that particular threat, maybe he could start to act like a normal man trying to win over the woman he might have feelings for. Whether she'd be interested in that was still an open question.

But for now, he had to shove all of that aside and focus on holding everybody together.

"Aunt Claudia needs our help cleaning up." He glanced at a truck as it pulled into the circular driveway. Raymond and Denise were finally coming back. "We need to get organized. We can wring our hands later. Right now let's get back inside."

Olivia finally walked through the door, hesitating only slightly at the threshold. She squared her shoulders and said, "Where do you want me to start?"

SEVENTEEN

A couple hours later Olivia couldn't get rid of the chill that had taken over her body.

The living room windows had been boarded up. Jonathan had made a quick trip to the store and returned with cleaning supplies and a boxful of lightbulbs, so the lights inside the house were mostly back to normal. And someone had turned on the furnace to heat up the downstairs rooms.

But none of that had managed to warm Olivia, who still felt ice-cold, even though she'd been busy cleaning alongside Claudia for a while now.

Try as she might to appear focused, calm and resolute, inside Olivia couldn't stop thinking chilly, frightening thoughts. Thoughts of a battered woman in Las Vegas, an innocent man in the hospital here in Painted Rock and Claudia's home defiled. She was losing the fight. Everyone good was losing the fight. Right now it looked like evil was winning.

"Here you go, honey." Claudia, ever the observant, considerate soul, dropped a heavy sweater over Olivia's shoulders. It smelled like hay and kitty kibble. "It does feel a little chilly in here, doesn't it?"

"Yes." Olivia forced herself to smile. "Thanks."

The deputies were gone and the houseful of remaining helpers had fanned out. Most of them were in the kitchen, dealing with that powdery, sticky nightmare coating the floors. Maybe that's where Elijah was. She hadn't seen him in a while, which was a good thing. Watching him walk through the house, emotionless and unaffected, as if everybody had just stopped by for a little spring-cleaning, made her angry every time she looked at him.

Maybe he could turn off his feelings when they were inconvenient. Good for him. She wasn't the same way and she resented his implication that she just needed to pull herself together.

She swept harder.

What made her truly furious was realizing he was right. When she looked at Claudia keeping a stiff upper lip, how could she do anything else but follow her lead? As they worked their way through sweeping the living room, she found herself both wondering where Elijah was and wanting him to stay far away at the same time.

She didn't want to be strong, didn't want to

hold herself together, didn't want to keep going. But it felt as if Elijah Morales was making her do just that.

She swept together a pretty good pile of glass and some dirt from an upended potted plant, then loaded the mess into a dustpan and emptied it all into a trash bag.

When she turned around, she saw Claudia standing completely still and staring at the ground.

"Aunt Claudia?"

She didn't answer. Olivia walked over to see what she was looking at.

It was a picture frame. The glass had been deliberately stomped, the picture torn underneath.

"That's Uncle Hugh," Olivia said. She reached down to pick it up, but Claudia put out her hand to stop her.

And then Olivia saw the shape of a flower that had imprinted itself on the glass. It was *that* picture. The one with the flower Claudia's husband of fifty-two years had picked and given to her in a silly gesture of love on his last day on earth.

The flower, already dry and brittle after the passage of time, now looked like a mere circle of dust. Like an ancient artifact from a long-forgotten time, it would vanish the moment someone touched it.

Olivia swallowed thickly, trying to choke back

her cold, hollow feelings of hopelessness, and desperately trying to think of something she might say or do to help.

The bare wooden floor squeaked as someone walked into the room.

"What's up?" Elijah asked, coming up behind them. Then he saw the picture on the floor. "Oh." He hesitated slightly, then put an arm around Claudia's shoulder and bumped his head lightly against hers. "I'm so sorry the jerk who did this destroyed your picture. But you know, if Hugh were here he'd laugh at you for getting so worked up over a dried-up old flower."

"Can't you show a little compassion?" Olivia asked tightly. His emotionless behavior added to her bottled-up aggravation.

"My Hugh was an odd mixture of practical and impractical, wasn't he?" Claudia said quietly.

Elijah nodded. "If he were here, he'd tell me to sweep up the mess and tell you to go get a new flower." Elijah took the broom from her hands but he didn't start sweeping.

"You risk so much when you love something—or someone," Claudia said. She finally looked up from the broken picture, her eyes damp with tears.

Olivia felt a wobbly sensation in the center of her chest.

"I really am sorry your picture got broken," Elijah said to Claudia, his voice husky. "But this house is full of good memories of Hugh. If you try to hang on to this broken glass and dust, they'll just remind you of the night some idiot tried to take those good memories away from you."

"You're right." Claudia sighed deeply.

"Why don't you go see what they're doing in the kitchen? I'll help Olivia finish up out here."

"All right." Claudia took one last lingering glance at the broken frame and the flower, and then turned away.

"I've got to learn how to turn my emotions on and off like you do," Olivia spat out after Claudia left. "That's got to be convenient."

He tilted his head slightly. "Want to know a secret?"

"What?"

"I don't turn them on and off. I put them away so I can take care of things for the moment. I let myself feel things later. That's how I'm wired and I suppose it is convenient. But I don't recommend it."

He started to sweep. Olivia watched him and thought about how much weight he willingly carried on his shoulders. She'd taken for granted that the things he did were easy for him. She'd gone out of her way to be annoyed with him because it was so much easier than feeling as if she was falling in love with a man who never seemed to let himself feel anything at all. Certainly nothing like love. And certainly not for her.

But that was probably all for the best. They'd been through a lot together, but he still had his unyielding sense of duty. And she still had one mess of a life she needed to clean up.

As the evening wore on, a few more people from Vanquish the Darkness arrived at Claudia's house to help with the cleaning. They brought hot food, dry goods to help restock Claudia's pantry, and assorted blankets and sheets to place over the ripped upholstery.

Mark and Linda rounded up a couple of other people to walk the grounds and make sure the horses were okay and no one was lurking in the barns or sheds. Raymond went with them and discovered the vandal had also struck the cottage.

It was all very helpful, but Elijah needed them to go home. *Now.* He nearly growled aloud. The shooter had intensified his game. Elijah needed to intensify his own efforts to catch the creep. He also needed to have a couple of potentially unpleasant conversations with people who actually lived in this house. That was hard to do with half the town jammed into the kitchen.

At the moment he and Bobby were the only people in the living room. Now that most of the lights were back on, the swinging door between the dining area and the kitchen was no longer propped open. It was actually quiet enough that he could think.

Bobby tapped away on his tablet, doing some research Elijah had assigned him. While waiting for him to finish, Elijah's dark thoughts turned to Olivia. She'd grown unnaturally pleasant and agreeable since their conversation after seeing the torn picture of Hugh with the crushed flower. Her demeanor felt false to Elijah. Whatever emotion Olivia felt, whether happy, sad or ready for a fight, it typically showed on her face. She expressed herself straightforwardly. That was one of the things that made him comfortable around her. Made him trust her.

He still trusted her. But he was also afraid for her. Underneath that slightly cynical facade she liked to show the world lay a warm, open, generous-hearted woman who cared deeply for others. He didn't want her to close any of that off, or hide it behind a false front.

He'd blown it when he hurried her into pulling herself together when they were out on the front porch. He still thought that it was a good idea to get her working, but he should have handled it better. Maybe listened to her for a little while. Now she was hiding something from him, and he very much wanted to know what it was.

"I've got everything we talked about in the shopping cart," Bobby said, looking down at his electronic tablet. "Do you want to pay for next-day delivery? It's going to cost a bundle."

Elijah nodded. "Do it."

"Okay." Bobby tapped the screen several times. "Done. Your entire security-camera system should be here tomorrow."

"Thanks."

"No problem." Bobby tapped the screen a couple more times. "As a token of your thanks, you just bought me a mystery novel I've really been wanting to read, too." He lay the tablet down on the arm of his chair. "So, are we staying here tonight?"

"You head on home whenever you're ready."

"I've got nowhere else to be."

"I need you to get some good sleep so you can hook up the system when it gets here." Elijah deliberately lightened his tone. He had plans for this evening. Potentially dangerous plans. He wanted Bobby safe at his own home tonight.

Elijah got to his feet. Maybe by the time he got to the kitchen he'd be able to think of a polite way to tell the remaining visitors it was time to go.

Fortunately, his dad walked in from the kitchen at about the same time. "What are you boys doing out here?"

"We ordered a security system for Aunt Claudia," Elijah said. "I just have to convince her she wants it before it gets here."

Joe sighed and looked around. "After all of this, maybe she'll agree to do it."

"I want her and Olivia to stay at the ranch tonight."

Joe raised an eyebrow. "You coming, too?"

Elijah shook his head. "I need you or Mom to take my truck home."

"You want it to look like no one's here?" Bobby asked.

"Yes. After this house-repair party *finally* winds down, I'm going to replace a couple of the outside lightbulbs now that the storm has passed and it's safe to put up a ladder. Then I'll close up the place so it looks empty."

"But you'll be here waiting." Bobby said.

"Whoever did this is probably watching the house right now. He sees all these people showing their support and trying to put things back to rights. What better way to break Olivia's spirit than to sneak back tonight and tear it all up again? Make the damage even worse the second time."

"But we'll be waiting for him," Bobby said.

Elijah looked at Bobby, grateful for the gift of such a loyal friend, even if he couldn't accept the offer of assistance. "*I'll* be waiting. It'll be easier and safer if I only have to worry about myself."

"Why don't we ask Sheriff Wolfsinger to have one of his deputies watch the house?" Joe said, a worried expression drawing a crease in his brow.

"We're a small town in a big county. You know he doesn't have enough manpower to have someone watch an empty house all night."

"Probably not."

What if this kept dragging on until Olivia took off on her own and got hurt again? Or killed? Elijah was afraid that's what she'd decide to do. He thought of Mrs. Somerset back in Afghanistan.

"*I* have to take care of this, Dad, and I just want to get it done. Would you go back in the kitchen and get Mom to leave? Maybe that will get everybody else moving. And let Aunt Claudia, Olivia, Raymond and Denise know I need to talk to them."

"I'll do that. But you and I will talk later. You aren't staying here alone." He held up a hand as Elijah started to argue. "Son, you are *not* doing this on your own."

Joe turned and walked back through the swinging door. Elijah heard him holler, "All right people, let's wrap this up and move out. We've been here long enough." Like his son, Joe Morales wasn't exactly known for his subtlety.

People started spilling out from the kitchen, Olivia among them. Elijah couldn't take his eyes off her. She and Denise were deep in conversation. Olivia looked down and nodded, her focus on a topic obviously important to her. Denise leaned in close, gesturing with her hands and speaking intensely.

Elijah wasn't above eavesdropping, but the hubbub of the group as they headed for the front door drowned out their conversation.

Olivia glanced over and their eyes met. She raised her eyebrows slightly, her expression hopeful, but also haunted. All evening he'd ached to take her in his arms, never more so than now. He wanted to chase away everything that worried her and help her understand there were still good things ahead in her life.

The second their gazes locked, Elijah felt so connected to her it was hard to believe there was ever a time when they hadn't know each other. He needed to tell her how he felt. And yet in that same moment he saw her expression close down. She glanced away and then looked back at him.

This time she wore a polite, distant smile. It was as if she'd slammed a door in his face.

Fifteen minutes later, all of the visitors were gone except for Bobby. Even Jonathan had left for the Morales house to help prepare for their overnight guests. Elijah still wanted to talk to Olivia alone, but first things first. He needed to sell Claudia on the idea of the security system.

Bobby hadn't moved from the chair he'd padded with thick, folded blankets and plopped down into when he'd first arrived. Now Denise and Olivia were sitting on the sofa which had also been padded with blankets. Claudia was sitting in a plain wooden chair, her hands tightly clamped on the arms as if she was trying to command the world to stay still.

Raymond stood muttering about all the cleanup he still had to do before he'd get to go to bed.

"I've ordered a security-camera setup for your house," Elijah said to Claudia. He hadn't been able to think of a way to ease into the topic. "If you hate it, I can send it back. But maybe you could give it a try."

"Under surveillance in your own home?" Raymond asked with a sneer. "What kind of life is that?"

It sounded a lot like Claudia's objection when

Elijah had originally brought up the subject. He frowned at Raymond. *Thanks for that.*

"It's not an invasion of your privacy," Bobby said calmly. "No one will see the recordings. You control everything. You can keep every scrap of information here, or have it stored in the cloud where it'll be secure and encrypted."

"The cloud?" Claudia repeated a little dazedly.

"You really think it'll be secure?" Raymond demanded. He looked around the room. "Doesn't anybody else around here follow the news?"

Elijah took a breath. Getting frustrated wouldn't help.

Olivia came to his rescue. She walked over to Claudia, stood behind her and placed her hands on her aunt's shoulders. "This won't go on forever. I promise. But you can just have the cameras set up outside. Nothing will record inside your house."

Raymond made a scoffing sound.

"I'll show you all the camera angles after I install it," Bobby said. "You can pick what works for you."

"All right." Claudia rubbed her hands together. "We'll try it."

Elijah looked at Olivia. "Thanks."

She responded with a slight nod.

He blew out a little exhale of relief. Two objectives down. One more to go.

EIGHTEEN

Olivia was interested in hearing what else Elijah wanted to talk about, but his phone rang and he glanced at the screen. "It's Deputy Bedford," he said. "Everybody wait here for a few minutes. I'll be right back." He walked off into the kitchen to take the call.

"It's getting late and I've still got a lot to do," Raymond groused. He suddenly stood. "I'm going to get started on some of the repairs in the cottage. We got the busted lock on the front door fixed and all that garbage that was strewn around the front room cleaned up, but there's still plenty more to do. Come get me if it looks like I'm going to miss anything important."

"Sit down," Claudia commanded. "He said he'd be right back."

Raymond sat.

Olivia caught Raymond and Denise sharing an annoyed glance. Who could blame them? They'd signed on to take care of a house and the grounds for a retired rancher and look what they'd gotten dragged into, thanks to her.

Elijah was back a few minutes later. "Good news. The FBI profiler just arrived in Phoenix. She'll be in Painted Rock tomorrow evening."

Olivia felt a genuine smile cross her lips. "I'm so glad to hear that."

"Bedford also said he tried to call you but your phone kept going to voice mail."

"Oh." She pulled it out of her pocket, suddenly remembering that she'd turned it off at the festival. She powered it back on.

"So what is it you needed to tell us?" Raymond asked impatiently.

Elijah moved one of the torn dining table chairs so he could sit next to Claudia. "I need everybody to stay at my house tonight. Maybe for a couple of nights. Just until we're sure your house is secure."

No, not tonight. Olivia's heart hammered in her chest as she stared at her feet, trying to compose herself. It was wonderful that the FBI profiler was almost here. But over the course of the evening she'd decided to remove herself from Claudia's life until everything was resolved. She'd planned to slip out of the house very early tomorrow morning without any emotional fanfare and head back to Vegas. She would have one of Painted Rock's few taxis pick her up from the road to take her to the airport and she'd immediately send a text so no one would worry about her.

Vanessa was a well-known attorney with enemies of her own, so she lived in a very secure building in Vegas. She'd given Olivia an open invitation to stay there.

She'd been certain she had no future in Las Vegas when she'd left, but maybe she was wrong. She'd already lost her one chance at a meaningful job in Painted Rock. Maybe she could find another opportunity in a bigger city.

"I guess we could stay at your place tonight if you really think it's important," Claudia said to Elijah. Having her home invaded must have understandably changed her priorities.

Olivia looked up, surprised and uncertain. There could be no slipping away unnoticed on the Morales ranch.

"You don't seem too worried about us," Denise said snidely.

"I meant to include you, too," Elijah said.

"No, thanks." Raymond crossed his arms tightly across his chest. "I think we'd be more comfortable at a motel." He looked pointedly at Claudia.

"Don't worry. I'll pay for it." She stood up. "But right now I'm going upstairs to get my doggies. They need to go outside and I need some air."

"Bobby, can you go with her when she goes outside?"

"Sure."

"Let's go back to the cottage," Raymond said to Denise, heading for the swinging door to the kitchen. "Maybe we can get something done before we have to leave."

"Let me take a quick look around the yard before you and Claudia go out," Elijah said to Bobby. He walked out the front door. Olivia got up and followed him outside.

The rain had stopped, but the breeze was still blowing in unsteady bursts. A full moon cast silver light between heavy storm clouds. Olivia tucked her windblown hair behind her ears and looked for Elijah in the darkness.

He melded into the shadows so completely that it took her a moment to find him. He was standing on the porch. Watching her.

Nerves danced in the center of her chest as she walked over to him. They'd been alone together many times before, but this time it felt different.

Another cloud passed overhead. After it was gone, the world was bathed in silver again. This time she could see the intense expression on his face and the light reflecting in his eyes.

"Are you all right?" he asked.

How many times had he asked her that? He was always checking with everyone else, making sure they were okay.

"I'm fine." Nerves got the better of her and she couldn't say anything more despite the questions that lay heavy on her heart. Was there any reason for her to stay in Painted Rock? One that involved a future with Elijah? Should she ignore the signals he'd started to send over the past few days and believe that he still meant to face the rest of his life alone?

Elijah pushed away from the side of the house where he'd been leaning and walked closer to her. He reached out to brush aside the hair that had already been blown loose and was back hanging in her eyes again. The warmth of his touch soothed her jangling nerves and sent them out of control at the same time.

"I can't stop you from leaving," he said. "But I wish you wouldn't go."

How did he know? She glanced at the boarded front window. "It's getting too dangerous around here. I think it would be best for everybody."

He moved closer, looked down into her eyes and rested his calloused hand against her cheek. "I don't want you to go," he said softly, leaning toward her until their lips were nearly touching and their breaths began to mingle.

The joyful yelp of a dog echoed inside the house. More yelps followed.

The front doorknob rattled and Olivia took a step back from Elijah. He smiled slightly but didn't move away.

The door opened and three wiggling dogs made a beeline across the porch and down the steps to the grass.

Claudia and Bobby walked out behind them. Claudia glanced skyward, and then headed down the steps behind her dogs.

"Hey, it's actually kind of nice out here now." Bobby paused on the porch and let the wind toss around his red curls.

"It is." Olivia tried to look anywhere but at Elijah. If she looked at him she'd be even more confused.

"You should probably go back inside," Elijah said, reaching out to touch her hand.

He smiled at her and she felt a warm blush heat her skin.

"Whoever did this to your aunt's house is probably watching. I don't want to take any chances."

"Me, neither." Getting shot at twice in her life was more than enough.

"Bobby, why don't you go back inside with her? I'll stay with Aunt Claudia. After she goes back in, I'll stay out here and get a few of these outside lights working. We'll head home as soon as I'm done."

"Okay." Bobby pulled open the door and gestured for Olivia to walk ahead of him.

As she stepped over the threshold, her phone chimed. A text from Denise:

Sorry Ray and I were so grouchy. Stressed and taking it out on other people. No excuse. Sorry.

Olivia texted back: Totally understandable. She started up the stairs. If they were going to the Morales place, she'd need to pack a few things. Her thoughts drifted to Elijah and that near kiss just now on the porch. Did he truly have room in his life for her? Or was it just the moonlight and the moment? Elijah Morales was tough and disciplined. But he was human, too.

Her phone chimed. Another text from Denise:

That jerk who tore up Claudia's house really did a number on the cottage. What a mess.

Olivia texted back: Need some help cleaning up? It wouldn't take long to pack. Besides, now that the guests were gone and the house was quiet, her nervous, jittery feeling was coming back. The person who shot her had been in this very house. He was circling closer. Maybe, despite everyone's best efforts, there wouldn't be a happy ending. Helping Denise would keep her mind occupied and away from morbid thoughts.

She looked down at her phone. Her hands were trembling. She tried to take a deep breath, but her lungs felt locked. She was on the verge of panic. She'd been out there on that uncertain edge of life so often lately she'd learned to recognize the signs.

Denise still hadn't texted back yet. She was probably up to her elbows in a bucket of soapy water. Might as well just walk over there. Elijah was outside keeping an eye on things, so she should be fine.

To be safe, she sent Denise a text telling her she was coming so she'd be on the lookout for her. She went downstairs. Bobby wasn't in the living room, but the TV was on in the den. He must be in there. "I'm heading out to the cottage," she called out to him.

She heard him say something, so she figured he'd heard her. With all her bases covered, she headed out the kitchen door to the cottage. Surely a little company and something useful to do would help her relax. If not, she didn't know how she'd be able to sleep tonight.

Elijah twisted a bulb into an exterior light fixture with grim determination. Every now and then he'd look around, certain he felt eyes raking over him, but he couldn't see anyone.

The wind continued to blow in fits and gusts, the clouds still sailing on the rough seas overhead. Moonlight would shine through the cloud breaks, but in the next instant it would be swallowed by darkness.

He climbed down off the ladder and listened. The wind whispered furiously as it wrestled through the treetops. Closer to the ground, branches in the trees and bushes rustled.

It was a good night to sneak up on someone. The restless wind offered a variety of noises to cover quiet footfalls.

It was a perfect night for a tracker like him to run down his prey, too.

Elijah was thankful Claudia and Olivia had agreed to go to his house. In a minute, he'd round everybody up and drive them over to the Morales ranch in one of Claudia's cars. He'd send Raymond and Denise to a hotel at the same time. Before he left he'd lock up the house, leaving a few lights burning inside and out, as someone would do if they were leaving for the night.

But he would come back. On foot. Under the cover of some nice, unsettling weather. He took a breath, enjoying the scents of damp pine and sage. The smell was fresh and clean and energizing. Finally having the chance to *do* something rather than waiting for the next attack was invigorating. A slight smile played at the corners of his lips.

His plan had changed since he'd talked to Bobby. Elijah wasn't going to wait inside. On a night as perfect as this, he'd wait outside. He'd watch the house and see who showed up. If his dad insisted on coming along, he could wait and watch, too.

In the army, and sadly in his work with Vanquish, Elijah had experience with people who fed off fear. They felt empowered by it. The creep who was after Olivia would see the house closed up as evidence he'd successfully scared her away for the night. He'd also see the opportunity the empty house presented to torment her again.

Elijah would be waiting. The shooter would be surprised. And then it would be over. Olivia would finally be safe. The fear that hounded her would be gone.

He walked around the house, glancing up at the upstairs bedroom windows, glad to see Claudia and Olivia had followed his directions and kept the shutters pulled together and the lights turned down low.

His phone rang. He glanced down at the screen. Olivia was calling. His heart melted like butter. Nothing he could do about that.

"Hey, what's up?"

"Elijah! We need your help!" Her words sounded frantic and choppy as if she couldn't catch her breath. Layered atop her voice, he could hear someone else yelling in the background, a woman. "No! No! Stop!"

Every cell in his body snapped to full attention. He reached for the gun tucked in the waist of his jeans and started at a run for the house, looking up at the lit windows, searching out shadows that looked menacing, listening for the shouts he could hear through the phone. "Where are you?" He was at the front porch. Where was Bobby? If the shooter had gotten to Olivia, he must have overpowered Bobby.

"The cottage!"

The cottage? What was she doing back there?

He changed direction, running back down the steps and around the house. "Are you all right?" He shouted into the phone. "Are you hurt?"

"No. But we need you here."

"I'm almost there. Tell me what's happening." Did he need more weapons? Did he need to come in through the window?

"It'll be okay," he heard her say in a shaky voice, talking to someone else.

"Is he there?" Elijah demanded, reaching the cottage, and then slowing down, pressing himself against the building, waiting for her intel to let him know how to approach the situation. "Is the shooter there?" The lights hadn't been re-placed back here. Darkness would give him good cover. The storm clouds were bunching together again and a light rain started to fall.

"No, he's not here now. But he was just here." Olivia's voice got shakier and it sounded as if she had turned away from the phone—maybe she was looking around. "At least, I don't think he's here." She spoke to someone else. "Could he still be here?"

Heart pounding in his chest, Elijah took a steadying breath and listened. He had one chance to move events in the right direction. This was where his training kicked in. Every fiber of his being wanted to rush in and save Olivia, but the best, most heartfelt intentions could get everyone killed. Sometimes you had to will your blood to turn to ice, make yourself slow down for a sec-ond and *think*.

He heard Olivia calling out his name inside the cottage. He heard her voice through his phone, too, sounding fearful and panicky. Much as he wanted to reassure her, he couldn't just yet.

The front door of the cottage was slightly ajar. Staying hidden behind the door, he pushed it open a little bit farther.

Darkness filled the living room at the front of the cottage. Just beyond it a faint glow lit the passageway to the kitchen. A bedroom lined up behind it at the back of the small building.

By the light of a small bedside lamp, he saw Denise bound to a wooden chair with wide strips of gray duct tape.

Olivia stood beside her, phone in one hand, using her other to tug helplessly at the tape.

Denise, tears streaming down her face, arms pinned to her sides, eyes wide with fear, kept yelling to Olivia in a hoarse voice, "No! Hang up and go! Just *go!*" A short curl of tape sat by her feet. Olivia had probably just pulled it from Denise's mouth.

Elijah silenced his phone, tucked it into his jeans pocket and started a slow, careful walk into the dark living room. He peered into the corners as best he could, taking advantage of the weak light spilling from the bedroom. He listened, trying to feel if there was anyone lurking in the shadows, all the while fighting the demand of his heart that he run straight to Olivia and make sure she was okay.

Farther into the living room he got a better view of the bedroom. The window was broken. The room had been tossed, leaving bedding and clothes everywhere. Denise tried to twist in her chair to face Olivia. She was still shouting at her to go.

"Where are you?" Olivia wailed into her

phone. At the same time she turned toward the front of the cottage and saw Elijah.

She ran to him, threw her arms around him and pressed her face into his chest.

He wrapped an arm around her while looking over her head. He wanted to feel relieved that she was safe in his arms, but he couldn't. An uneasy feeling still squirmed in his gut. He hadn't searched the whole cottage yet.

Olivia suddenly let go of him, then grabbed his hand and pulled him toward Denise. "He was here!" She looked pale and frightened, her eyes wide. "Ted Kurtz was just here!"

NINETEEN

Elijah glanced down at Denise, still taped to the chair, strode into the kitchen to grab a knife from a wooden block to cut her free, and then came back.

"Ted Kurtz was *here*," Olivia said more forcefully. Elijah hadn't reacted to that terrifying news yet and she wanted to shake him.

She felt as if she was back in Vegas, still trapped in that world of fear Kurtz had created. All the healing she'd experienced since arriving in Painted Rock had vanished in an instant.

Kurtz had promised to catch her alone and kill her. Olivia looked at poor Denise. Now he'd added tormenting everyone around her to the mix.

Elijah took the knife and began sawing the bands of tape that bound Denise's hands.

In that horrifying moment when Olivia found Denise gagged and taped to the chair, her first thought had been to call Elijah. She'd torn the tape from Denise's mouth, and while Denise had cried out to her, wild-eyed and frantic, Olivia had focused only on hearing Elijah's voice. Now that he was here, Olivia could turn her attention back to what Denise was saying.

"Go!" Denise strained toward Olivia despite the strong tape holding her to the chair. "He's going to kill you. Get out. Leave town, *now*!"

"Who's going to kill her?" Elijah asked, sawing through the tape around Denise's legs while she rubbed her freed hands together.

"Ted Kurtz!" Denise practically screamed. "He was here!"

Olivia's breath froze in her lungs. She'd thought about the mob lawyer so much, feared him so much, that he'd become larger than life. A malevolent phantom.

But now he was here, in Painted Rock. Flesh and blood, and all too real. Lurking on Claudia's property. Maybe just outside the cottage. Or hiding inside it.

"We need to get out of here," she said as cold fear began a piercing climb up her spine.

Elijah stayed crouched by Denise, knife in his hand. "Are you sure it was Kurtz?" he asked Denise.

His calm, methodical manner was driving Olivia crazy. Didn't he understand the danger they were in? Didn't he understand they needed to get out, *now*?

"I've seen his picture. It was him." Denise stretched out toward Olivia, grasping at her with a damp, clammy hand. "He said if you stay he'll kill Claudia."

Olivia's stomach turned to stone.

"He'll go after everyone you care about. He'll kill Elijah, Joe, Julie, me, all of us." Hysterical, Denise started crying again. "You ruined his life and he said he'll ruin yours."

"How can he be here?" Olivia asked Elijah. Terror and confusion mixed crazily in her head. Was Kurtz really that good, that well connected? Had he tricked Homeland Security and the State Department? "Wouldn't Bedford tell us if he was back in the States?"

Elijah held her gaze. Then he shook his head very slightly.

"What?" Denise asked, looking dazed. "No, he was here. *Right here*. He broke through that window." She pointed to it. "He grabbed me, he taped me up and told me next time he would kill me. He said all of us are marked targets as long as you're here." Now she was pointing at Olivia.

"Where's Raymond?" Elijah asked.

"Outside. Repairing the lights."

"No, he isn't." His gaze shifted to the broken window, then back to Olivia. "Call Deputy Bedford," he said. "And tell him to keep an eye out for Raymond when he gets here."

"No!" Raymond shoved open the closet door and pointed a rifle at Elijah's head. "Put your hands where I can see them."

Olivia stared uncomprehendingly.

Elijah lifted his hands and started to stand.

"No! Stay right there."

"What?" Olivia turned to Elijah. "What's happening?"

Denise stood, all pretense of fear gone in an instant. She wiped away her false tears and pushed aside the tape Elijah had just cut through.

"What's going on?" Olivia asked.

Denise barely spared her a glance as she kicked aside the discarded tape on the floor and reached under the bed, pulling out a shotgun. "Things were going just fine until you showed up and decided to stay. Why didn't you just visit for a week and leave like a normal relative?" She pointed the shotgun at Olivia. "You didn't care about the old lady. She had to hire us, complete strangers, to help her with this place. We deserve to inherit it more than you do. We've been more family to her than you have."

"We could kill Olivia and tell the sheriff we saw someone shoot her and run off toward the forest," Raymond mused aloud. "We'd just need to wait a few more months to kill Claudia. To throw off suspicion."

Denise nodded toward Elijah. "Yeah, but what about him?"

"We shoot him and tell the cops Kurtz killed both of them."

"Ted Kurtz is here?" Olivia asked, voice trembling.

Denise rolled her eyes. "Who knows where Ted Kurtz is? Who cares?" She glanced at Raymond and ratcheted her shotgun. "Are we gonna do this?"

A sudden tug on Olivia's hand brought her crashing to the floor while at the same time Elijah sprang up past her, the glinting blade of the knife in his hand flashing as he lunged toward Raymond.

Olivia's forehead smacked the ground and for a few seconds she lay dazed. Wrenching herself back to the here and now, she recognized the sounds of a struggle.

"Elijah!" He only had a knife. Raymond had a rifle. Denise had that shotgun.

Frantic to help, she turned toward Elijah just in time to see Denise swing the butt of the shotgun toward her. Olivia jerked her head back at the last second but still got clipped on the chin, the force of the blow knocking her back flat on the floor.

A rifle shot fired, sounding horribly loud in the small room. The mirror over the dresser exploded.

"Elijah!"

The room shifted uneasily through her blurred vision as she flattened her palms on the floor and pushed herself up. Elijah and Raymond were still grappling, shoved halfway into the closet, trading kicks and punches.

Denise, standing near Olivia, sneered and swung her foot to kick Olivia in the head.

Summoning every ounce of strength she had, Olivia reached up and grabbed Denise's foot and pulled.

Denise landed flat on her back, hard. Her shotgun clattered to the floor. She rolled to her side and reached for it.

Quickly crawling forward despite her dizziness, Olivia's fingers reached the cold metal near the trigger and shoved hard. The gun slid beneath the bed.

With a feral growl, Denise crawled after it.

Olivia pushed herself up onto the balls of her feet and sprang after her, only to be caught around the waist before she left the ground.

Screaming and flailing, she wrenched around to find Elijah had grabbed hold of her. He grunted and shifted her to his side, encircling her body with an arm that felt as strong and solid as granite. He stepped forward and pressed a booted foot into the center of Denise's back, stopping her from crawling any closer to the shotgun. "Don't move," he said, pistol in his free hand. "I don't want to shoot you, but I will."

Olivia looked toward the closet. Raymond lay crumpled and unconscious. When she turned back she saw Elijah was bleeding.

"You're shot!" She tried breaking free to get a better look at his injury, but he wouldn't loosen his grip. "I'm all right," he said, breathing hard. His black eyes were deep wells of controlled rage. And then they softened with compassion. "It's okay," he said more gently. "We're both all right."

She blew out a breath and let herself melt into the crook of his arm.

"Elijah!" It was Bobby's voice.

"Back here!"

Bobby cautiously peered around the corner of the open cottage door and into the bedroom, phone in one hand and pistol in the other. He looked first at Olivia, then at Denise and Raymond. Finally his gaze settled on Elijah and the growing bloom of blood in the side of his shirt. "You need an ambulance."

"I don't need an ambulance," Elijah said to Bobby. He glanced at Raymond, happy to see he still lay unmoving on the closet floor. "He grabbed my pistol and got off a shot that hit the dresser mirror. It didn't hit me."

Olivia stepped away from him and looked pointedly at the blood on his shirt. "Nothing to worry about," Elijah assured her. "He managed to give me a slight scrape with the kitchen knife, that's all."

He turned his gaze back to Denise. She was still on the floor, his foot still on her back to keep her from reaching the shotgun under the bed. Enraged, she cursed and shouted threats. No one was listening to her. "Just call the cops, Bobby."

"I already did. When I couldn't find you or Olivia, I knew something was wrong. "His eyes were wide. "I'm so sorry, Elijah." He turned to Olivia. "When did you come out here?"

"You didn't hear me call out to you?"

"No. I had the TV on, and then I was talking on the phone. When I finished my call, I looked for you. Then I looked for Elijah. When Aunt Claudia told me she didn't know where either one of you were, I figured I'd better call Bedford." He turned back to Elijah. "I can't believe this. What happened?"

"I'll explain everything when the cops get here. In the meantime, help me with this." Elijah pointed to the roll of tape that had been used on Denise. While he kept his foot on her, he had

Bobby tape her hands together and then her feet before doing the same to Raymond, who was starting to regain consciousness.

Blue lights flashing through the open door of the cottage announced the arrival of Bedford and a couple other deputies.

Bedford called for a medic despite Elijah's protests. Olivia insisted he let the paramedic check out his injury and sat beside him in the back of the ambulance. Once his shirt was off, he had to admit to a little more than a scrape. The truth was Raymond had managed to get the knife away from him and plant it fairly deeply in Elijah's side. But then Elijah knocked him out, so it was all good.

"The tape will hold you for now," the medic said after slathering him with an antibiotic gel, "but you'll want to get some stitches."

"You'd better do it," Olivia threatened.

"Yes, ma'am." Elijah looked down at her tense, yet smiling face beside him. She was a strong woman. She'd proven that over and over. It was good to know he could count on her to keep her head in a tough situation. Even better to know he could lean on her when he needed to.

"You did all right back there," he said, reaching out to trace a finger across her cheek. "You been in a lot of bar fights or something?"

She laughed and looked down at her torn, disheveled clothes. "I've never been in an actual physical fight before." She looked up at him with a proud, cockeyed grin. "That was my first."

"You did good. I'm scared of you now."

Her grin widened. "Thanks."

She was quiet for a few minutes. The paramedic and EMT were outside the rig, holding clipboards and finishing some paperwork. "You all right?" he asked as he jostled her slightly with his arm.

She smiled at him and his heart did a slow, lazy dance. "I'm actually doing okay at the moment, thanks for asking." She rubbed her hands together as if trying to warm them. "I might have a tough time later, though, when things calm down and I have time to think. But I'll get over it."

"That's how I live my life." Elijah knew the pattern well. Faith helped him through. And family.

"All that time fighting overseas?" she asked softly. "You'll always have the aftermath of that to deal with, won't you?"

He nodded. "I think so."

She took in a deep breath and blew it out. "I could live with that. If we talked about things that were bothering you. Prayed about them. Got help if we needed it. We could be good for each other."

A delicate ache warmed his heart. Something so different from all the physical pain he'd felt. This was an emotional pang. Something he hadn't let himself feel for a very long time. His closed heart was opening and he was letting it, even though it meant he could end up getting hurt. Or, worse than that, even if it meant he could hurt someone else. Not that he would intentionally hurt Olivia. Ever.

"Does this mean I don't have to worry about you running off after all?" he asked.

She grinned. "I'll stay long enough for you to heal up and give me a ride on that chrome beast you call a motorcycle. If you want me to stay longer than that, you're going to have to charm me."

He leaned over to brush his lips against hers. She released a tiny sigh and he wrapped his arm around her waist to pull her closer.

Claudia popped her head in the back of the ambulance. "Kids! Tell me you're okay!"

"More than okay," Olivia murmured.

Two of Claudia's chubby little dogs managed to jump into the back of the rig and give Olivia and Elijah a worried sniff.

Both Elijah and Olivia reached out to give them a reassuring pat.

"Would you mind calling my parents and telling them everything's okay?" Elijah asked Claudia. "They probably have their scanner on and I'm sure they're worried."

"Of course. I'll do that right now." She called her dogs out of the ambulance and they left in an excited, barking huddle.

"Let's get out of here, too." Elijah stood and clambered out of the rig. Then he held out his hand to help Olivia. Once she was out, he didn't let go of her hand.

Sheriff Wolfsinger rolled up in his patrol car. He stopped for a quick minute to make sure Elijah and Olivia were okay before heading to the cottage where Denise and Raymond had been separated and were being questioned.

A short time later, Deputy Bedford finally came out to talk to them. "We got a hit on a set of prints we took from the house earlier tonight," he told them. "They're for a woman with a criminal record in Utah. She was blonde and blue eyed in the mug shot, but now the resemblance is obvious."

"You're talking about Denise?" Olivia asked.

Bedford nodded. "Yeah. Though that's not her real name. She and her boyfriend, 'Raymond,' have been arrested several times for cons over the last ten years. More recently, they were suspects in the murder of an elderly woman they took care of. Just before she died, she changed her will and named them as sole beneficiaries to her estate. Her family was suspicious, asked for testing to be done and discovered her blood showed high levels of medicines her doctor had not prescribed for her."

Elijah felt a chill pass through him at the thought of what might have happened to Claudia.

"Denise told me Aunt Claudia had memory problems," Olivia said. "She was always pushing her to take some kind of special vitamins."

"Vitamins?" Bedford asked. "Did they make her sick? Change her level of consciousness?"

"Thankfully, I think she was too stubborn to ever take any of them," Olivia said.

Elijah gave her hand a squeeze.

"When the family of the elderly lady asked for a formal criminal investigation, 'Denise' and 'Raymond' disappeared," the deputy said.

Olivia turned to him. "So they were after Aunt Claudia's money from the moment they got here?"

"Until you showed up and ruined their plans. They'd heard about Claudia downsizing her ranching operation after Hugh's death from one of her former ranch hands. They asked a few questions, found out she didn't have any family hanging around and offered their services.

"Your aunt turned them down at first. But they convinced her she would need lots of help as she got older. Told her it would be more honorable to hire them than to expect her friends and neighbors to help her for free. They thought they'd found someone they could slowly poison with no one to get in their way."

Elijah turned to her. "You just might have saved her life by coming here."

"So far, we know Raymond drove you off the road hoping to scare you away. He shot you in the woods. He was the one who fired the shotgun, and then walked through the furniture store just as Elijah suspected. He had the shotgun under a long raincoat and no one thought to mention him to the deputies because they knew him.

"Denise started the fire." He looked at Olivia. "She thought you had gone back in the shed to do a little more cleaning."

Bedford took a deep breath and smiled grimly. "We should have all the specific details we need before the night is over. Sheriff Wolfsinger's told them the first one to fully confess will get a plea deal. They're ratting out each other as fast as they can."

"So Ted Kurtz had nothing to do with it?" Olivia asked.

"Apparently not. When Claudia started talking about your upcoming visit, Denise and Raymond did some research and found out what happened with you in Vegas. They didn't know

Kurtz had threatened you, but figured you'd be worried about him wanting revenge. As soon as they heard you were assuming it was Ted Kurtz who drove you off the road, they figured they were home free."

Bedford glanced at the house. "I'm going to go get those vitamins from your aunt so we can have them tested."

After Bedford walked away, Elijah wrapped his arm around Olivia's shoulder and pulled her close to his side.

"It's finally over," she said, wrapping her arm around his waist and hugging him tight.

He leaned over and kissed the top of her head. "Some things are over. Some things are just beginning."

TWENTY

Eight months later

"It's about time you married that girl," Arthur said to Elijah as he rolled his wheelchair over to him.

Olivia grinned. These days it seemed as if she either grinned or laughed all day long. They were in the art room at Golden Sands. A couple of weeks after the arrest of "Denise" and "Raymond," Larry had called Olivia to say he'd been given the authority to rehire her if she was interested. She'd immediately accepted the offer.

"The wedding is the day after tomorrow," Elijah reminded Arthur. "I expect you to be there."

"I thought maybe it was today because of the way you're dressed. Slacks, a dress shirt and a tie? I didn't think you owned anything besides jeans and a black leather jacket."

"Funny." Elijah reached out to squeeze his friend's frail shoulder. "We're on the way to our rehearsal dinner. Think you could save up some wisecracks for the wedding reception?"

"Oh, I'll have plenty to say there." He winked at Olivia before he started to roll away. "You look beautiful as always."

"Thank you."

Elijah reached for her hand and kissed it. She felt as if her whole body was glowing. "Are you going to be able to stand being away from your job for the next couple of weeks?" he asked.

"Arthur assured me he'll keep everybody in line."

"Good." Elijah flicked off the lights. "Let's lock this place up and get going."

Olivia looked out at the late-spring sunlight shining on the hills, highlighting all the brave bits of green poking out of the earth. Hard to believe just a few months ago she had looked out at those same hills with a heart full of fear.

"When I picked up Vanessa at the airport yesterday, she told me Ted Kurtz finally returned to Vegas, where he was arrested and charged with assault," Olivia said. "His ex-wife is finally willing to testify against him. Other charges will be filed soon. He isn't going to get away with all the terrible things he did."

"And Ricky's recovered and back at work." Elijah stepped up behind her, wrapped his arms around her and pulled her close to his chest. "So it really is over."

He brushed his warm lips against the side of her neck and she melted against him.

"Are you ready to go face a restaurant full of family and friends?" he asked.

"I am."

They locked up the classroom and walked out to Elijah's truck, their destination a steak house in town. Once there, Olivia didn't make a move to get out of the truck. Instead, she sat with her gaze resting on the row of shiny motorcycles in the parking lot.

"You change your mind?" Elijah asked after a few seconds. "Have you decided you don't want to marry me?"

Olivia shook her head. "No. It's just that my mom and her husband, plus my dad and his wife and their children are in there. Together. We've never all been together in the same room before. Usually, my parents can't even carry on a civil conversation over the phone."

Elijah reached over and brushed the hair from her face. "Whatever happens, we'll make the best of it." He kissed her cheek. "You've faced down someone trying to kill you. I think you can handle a family squabble if one pops up."

"True."

"My sister and older brother both made it into

town today so you're going to meet them plus a few other members of the Morales family. I might need some moral support, too."

Years ago, when she'd felt so lonely, she'd prayed to be surrounded by family. Now that prayer had been answered.

She had Elijah. Someone by her side when things got tough. Someone she could take care of when things got tough for him. A true partnership. The best gift of all.

"I'm ready," she said, opening the truck door. "Let's get started."

* * * * *

Dear Reader,

I came across the announcement for the Killer Voices contest just days before the entry deadline. I needed to write a suspenseful first page for a story and I immediately knew what the setting would be. I've driven cross-country several times, and each time I've found myself uneasy driving through those long stretches of beautiful, empty desert. What if I ran into trouble? What if my car broke down? What if someone with evil intent came along and there was no one around to help?

Yeah, I scared myself on those drives. I almost scared myself writing that first page, too.

My original idea turned into a story about someone in danger who feels very alone. But then help arrives! First in the form of a menacing-looking motorcycle group. Then in the form of an estranged family member. After that, complete strangers in a town she's never visited before step up to offer assistance.

We can't always see where our help will come from before it appears. In the Killer Voices contest, I received help from Elizabeth Mazer, an editor I'd never met before. Complete strangers in the Harlequin Community Forum offered encouragement and congratulations.

And, thank goodness, family and friends supported my efforts.

Olivia and Elijah couldn't see what form of help would show up before it appeared. They couldn't know when it would appear. But they trusted God and moved forward one step at a time.

Sounds like a good plan to me.

Jenna Night